JOE'S WORD

An Echo Park Novel

Elizabeth Stromme

City Lights Books
San Francisco

Cover photograph: Joshua Paul
Cover design: Stefan Gutermuth
Typography: Harvest Graphics

Library of Congress Cataloging-in-Publication Data

Stromme, Elizabeth.
    Joe's word : an Echo Park novel / Elizabeth Stromme.
        p.   cm.
    ISBN 0-87286-425-1 (alk. paper)
    1. Los Angeles (Calif.) — Fiction.   2. Writing services —
Fiction.   3. Inner cities — Fiction.   4. Immigrants — Fiction.
I. Title.
    PS3619.T775J64 2003
    813'.6 — dc21

                                                    2003012700

CITY LIGHTS BOOKS are edited by Lawrence Ferlinghetti and Nancy J. Peters and published at the City Lights Bookstore, 261 Columbus Avenue, San Francisco CA 94133.
Visit our web site: www.citylights.com

For Rae, Lili, and Linda

Echo Park c. 1995

Shadowed by an increasingly crowded downtown sky-line—hard by Dodger Stadium and Chinatown, at the wrong end of Sunset—the community of Echo Park was once L.A.'s first stylish suburb and a cradle for the young film industry moving West. Chaplin, Keaton, Fatty Arbuckle all worked there at one point, Keystone Kops careened through its steep streets, Laurel and Hardy heaved pianos up its famous steps nearby.

By 1995, though, Echo Park had long become inner city, and its upside mostly rundown. *Joe's Word* takes place in this transitional time window—before the scandal that turned Rampart into a household name for police corruption, before the Internet turned into spam, and "Russian brides" were another name for escort services.

Since the novel was completed in 1996, *Joe's Word* has been translated and published in France; Echo Park, too, has gone through some paces. The gentrification of neighboring Los Feliz and Silverlake has seeped in from the west, the Short Stop has gone from cop bar to hipster disco, and record stores, art galleries, and coffeehouses have arrived as well. Yet Echo Park retains its mixed immigrant population and still can be a tough area. The Jensen Recreation Center, to all appearances, remains unchanged.

Elizabeth Stromme
Echo Park, 2003

One

I was reaching for the Russian file when the pigeon flew in. It wasn't the first time. We both knew the drill.

Teresa tossed a plastic cover over the FAX and printer while I went for the computer and keyboard.

If you'd stop leaving out those . . ." I started to grouch, but Teresa was already out of hearing at her beauty shop next door getting a dirty towel from the hamper. And then what did it matter. You can't reason with pigeon feeders.

On its umpteenth circuit the bird smacked into a file cabinet.

"Bingo," I called out, tapping my foot, but Teresa was still gone and hell if I was going to throw my new sweater over the thing. By the time she'd returned it was too late: the eyes had blinked and turned wild again and then it was off, flailing on the ceiling, trying to beat a retreat. You'd have thought it'd try the window instead, or even the door, but pigeons have a reputation to uphold.

Bits of down sailed about the room and settled on our hair.

1

"Poor thing," Teresa said, adjusting her shawl. "He's lost his flock."

I didn't answer. I flicked a feather off my shoulder. Teresa's sense of community was one for the books. Pigeons. People. I wouldn't have been surprised if she'd had an ant farm as a child, if they had those things back where she was from. That was probably where she got her feelers. She had a pair of antennae on her, and they were always moving. It's not that I minded—they served her well at her place—but I'd asked her to turn them off whenever she came over to work for me.

It wasn't long before the pigeon fell for good. Teresa wrapped it in the towel and took it out to the sidewalk.

A little vacuuming and we were back at our desks.

I pulled out my good pen and stationery and started on Katia.

Hello Katia [I wrote],

I hope you will excuse me if this letter seems stiff. Although I'm at ease in a world of business transactions and am considered quite a go-getter, I'm afraid when I'm face-to-face socially with a lovely woman my self-assurance walks out the door. That is why I am writing you today. You are an exotic and beautiful young woman, I can see by your photograph. I am hoping that we can get to know each other by degrees and over time, and that through a gentle, warm and understanding partner, I can crack the shell of loneliness that prevents me from living a full and happy life.

Please do not think, though, that I'm strange. I'm good-natured. I love children and dogs. I'm not bad to look at, either, for fifty years of age. True, I have a narrow face. It looks like I squeaked through the birth canal. But otherwise I have a normal build and normal set of fingers and toes. I'm kind of hairy, too, but I'm no ape.

As for the work I mentioned above, I am the head of my own business, which is in the literary field. My office, in a building on Sunset Boulevard, is mostly home to professional tenants—antique dealers and the like. My home in the nearby hills features a classic-type garden in front, an important amenity for a man like me, for I have a sensitive side.

In some respects, yes, you could say I have it all: a late-model car, comfortable home, good career. But what I miss is a ribbon to wrap it up, a woman to fill the hollows of my days, to live and lie together.

I have tried, Katia, to write simply and from the heart. I hope that we speak the same language deep down and that the two of us can be two halves that meet, two pulses that beat by airmail.

> With much regard and anticipation,
> Will Brigham

I pulled out a glossy and tucked it in the envelope. Then I turned my top desk drawer inside out.

"We're out of stamps for Europe," I told Teresa.

She made a note of it and when she looked up, she reminded me again it was time to go over the books. "I've got a root perm tomorrow at two," she said, eyes locked on mine. "I can make it from three to five."

"All right," I mumbled.

I got up and stretched. "I guess I'm going to call it a day then." Teresa arched an eyebrow and glanced at her watch.

Sure, it was early for a go-getter, but not for an imposter. "Blame it on the pigeon, okay? I want to go home and roost."

"All alone?" she clucked under her breath.

I gave her ponytail a tweak. " 'Night, Teresa."

" 'Night, Joe."

I paused at the doorway to zip up my sweater. Days were starting to warm up, but nights were still fresh.

My other neighbor, the *dentista,* was on his doorstep, too. He was smoking a cigarette under his shingle, flashing a smile at anyone who happened by. He turned it on and he turned it off, he was his own neon sign. Even his clothes had flash. A set of gold chains glinted on his chest. His shiny shoes had tassels. It's not that I have a suspicious mind, but one exaggeration deserved another: I always wondered where he got the gold.

You could hear the whine of his machines from my office, and occasional sharp cries.

I stopped on Sunset to get some corn, that way I wouldn't have to cook vegetables tonight. I had to wait because the cobs needed more roasting, but I watched the vendor poke at the grill and time went by. It was rush hour. Sidewalk traffic backed up around us and the two children playing at our feet.

Manoukian was at the window of his pawn shop, taking it all in. He glared at me as I walked by.

A block beyond Sunset you could hear yourself think, or if nothing was playing, you could hear birds tweet. I got an earful—a full-blast rill was more like it—from a couple of mockingbirds on adjacent treetops. Of course I'd noticed (for I have my sensitive side): it was that time of the year for the birds and the bees. The leaves in the trees were putting on a show, too, covering the grids of telephone and electrical wires.

Plus all those young couples, hand-in-hand. More than buds were swelling.

I dropped my corncob in the gutter for some dog to finish off.

At the corner of Glendale I joined the locals lining the curb, shoulders forward, on their marks. With eight lanes of commuter traffic to cross on a green light, you had to be on your toes. I got ready, too, but I knew I'd make it, I'd been making it twice a day now for almost three years and I would've made it this time, too, except I got snared by a tottering old Italian who went for me like I was a life preserver. There was no thanks, not even eye contact, though that was okay with me. If he didn't like being dependent, I didn't like being pegged as a good egg.

Once I'd gotten over the shock of being requisitioned just like that, the two of us inched through the intersection, gazes fixed ahead, ignoring each other and the engines revving at our flanks.

When we reached the far side he let go his grip and we went our separate ways. I looked back once to see how he was doing.

He was peering into the coin return of a telephone booth, in a doughnut store parking lot.

I looked at my watch. Still plenty of time.

The lady halfway up the hill said hi like she always did, just like her dog always barked and lunged till she said shush. The lights below were starting to turn on, the carnicería, the

taco stand, the car wash. It was a pretty sight from a distance.
You could barely smell the fried fat from up here, especially
now with every green thing in bloom. In fact if you closed
your eyes and let yourself drift, you might've thought you
were in the tropics, the air was so perfumed. But I didn't. No
one would. You had to keep your eyes open in Echo Park.

I turned into a group of small bungalows bunched
around a scruffy courtyard. Suzette was on her stoop. I had
to step over her legs. She was waiting for the paint job on her
toenails to dry.

"Hi," I said.

"Hi."

I couldn't get past her tattoos.

A windfall avocado lay smashed on the walk. I kicked it
into the thatch that had claimed the flower bed.

Number 4's cat was at its post, staring out the front window. So was Number 4, in front of his TV. His TV was so big,
you could watch it from my living room. Above it hung one
of those factory clocks.

Next door, George was out.

I threw my mail onto the sofa and went straight to the
kitchen to thaw a patty and crack a beer. I had to put out the
garbage, too, it was garbage night, and sweep the ants out the
door, so it was 6:45 by the time I put on a record, shoved
aside a pile of books and stretched out on the floor. At last. I
wriggled my toes to the first notes of Bach.

Forty minutes later the day's muddle had dissolved and I
was where I wanted to be. Home. Home to the tonic. A
pleasant sizzle coming from the kitchen countered the

melancholy of the record's last cut. On the last note I lifted my head and smelled smoke.

I dashed to the kitchen, grabbed a potholder and flipped my sputtering burger onto a waiting bun. The meat was charred, I had to knock off the edges, and then the ketchup clogged till it broke loose. Yet I was philosophic about the mess on my plate. No homemade meal could ever match the real experience: the steamy hot dog of the stadium stands, with the sheen of Naugahyde.

7:28. Baseball season — opening game! Batter up.

Two strides and I was back in the living room, sunk in my armchair. I had to wait till the mist in my TV parted, but in the meanwhile I had the sound. Happy Days Are Here Again.

I took a swig of my second beer and hummed along.

What I like about baseball is its pace. Usually not much happens, either, and that's another plus. But tonight in the fourth inning a Dodger started a fight so I got up and drained my pipes, and when I got back peace had been restored. What a fine sport, I thought, with the generosity that comes with beer. The playing field was a picture: lush, flawlessly groomed, the color of fresh-minted money — except at the top right-hand corner of my screen, where the green fused with purple thanks to some screwy pixels.

I was used to the defect, it didn't bother me much, although sometimes it made me feel I was watching art.

After the game was over I did the dishes. It generally took me ten minutes to tidy up, including putting away the plates from the night before, but tonight it took longer because of the wall with the ketchup.

I took a book and my third beer to bed. I hadn't gotten far on either count when George's apartment came back to life. Normally George and his dog Sergeant didn't make much noise. Sergeant would scratch his fleas and thump the floor for ten minutes, but then it'd be lights out. But tonight there was an accompaniment to the ritual sound effects: the staccato of high heels. George had a date.

A glass fell and broke on the floor.

I kept my earplugs in the top drawer of my bedside table, and that's where they stayed. I set my book down on my chest, tucked my hands behind my head and waited. George usually scored.

George put on a goofy CD, and along with the goo came the giggles. The walls were wasp paper.

Her voice was high, tight. Young.

High heels. A redhead?

They were dancing toward the bedroom.

"Stay, Sergeant!" George commanded, closing the bedroom door behind them. The dog scratched at the wood and whined while they fell to it.

"Mm . . . mmft!"

"Oooooo."

George was banging the girl so hard the wall shook and the clock on my bedside table quivered. They were at it for a stretch. George was in his thirties and could drink hard and still get it on, but he couldn't always get off.

"Mm . . . mmm . . . mmft!"

"Oof!"

Some time after George and his date passed out, I picked

up my book again and resumed reading, but it wasn't long
before I caught myself nodding off, too. I was reading one of
my favorite Simenon's, but give me *War and Peace, The Story
of O,* it was all the same to me—it was always midnight
when my inner clock stopped.

A couple of hours later the helicopters came down.

It was the light that cracked through my dreams at first,
in flashes, like an optical nerve gone haywire. Then, on its
heels, the sound of rotor blades. I groaned when I realized
what was going on, a hairy groan, still groggy from sleep.
Someone was being chased.

You can run but you can't hide.

I groped for my earplugs, but they weren't there. Of
course not. The wax had gotten too grotty—I'd thrown
them out last week. The last pair in the box.

I pulled a pillow over my head and started to count to one
hundred, but I got bored fast. The helicopter was holding a
tight radius low over the block. Every thirty seconds the
apartment and everything in it vibrated from the percussion
of the blades—the windows, the lamps, my eardrums. I
didn't need a pillow, I needed a bunker.

A dog yelped nearby. I wasn't the only one rattled. I
squished my pillow around my head. With my one eye not
flattened against the mattress, I watched the show out of my
airhole. I didn't have much scope, but I could imagine. I'd
seen it before. They were using their candlewatts. Every
thirty seconds the cold white beam scoured the empty lot
next door before it moved off, down the line, over other
backyards and alley sheds. Reflections of the glare circled the

room. Every thirty seconds, a vortex of sound and light. Some people paid good money to experience this sort of thing—at the movies, at historic parks—but in the inner city you got it for free. I bit my lip and waited for the final curtain, but instead the search intensified.

Another chopper was coming. Sure! Up the ante!

Then the squad cars arrived.

"... AIR 22 ... BRA.CC. .CHT ... WHAT D'WE GOT HERE? ..."

"... RRRCH. .HT ..."

"... OKAY, GUYS, C'MON OUT ... WE'VE GOT DOGS ..."

Jesus Christ! I leaped out of bed, jerked open the window. A cop, passing under my window, shined his high beam on my face.

"Stay inside," he said.

Stay inside.

I grabbed a pillow and slammed it against the wall.

"Shut the fuck up!" yelled George from the other side. "I'm trying to sleep!"

Two

Jack Kramer was there, on the Sunset Sports Walk of Fame. So was Sandy Koufax, Parry O'Brien, and other dimming luminaries—if you could spot them through the layers of pigeon droppings and old wads of chewing gum. I walked this stretch every day on my way to work. I knew the sticky plaques. I knew the *roperias* and the Arab discount shops and the lines of day workers at the local hardware store. I knew the faded warnings, too, stenciled above the gutters by some Westside eco-group: NO DUMPING. THIS DRAINS TO OCEAN.

I looked into a gutter.

Chock full. I knew it.

I didn't feel so hot. I'd taken a tranquilizer after the pillow thing, and when that hadn't worked I'd popped a sleeping pill. I was late getting in to the office, but what the hell. Nothing there that couldn't wait.

Beanie was doing his number in front of the dead medical center. It wasn't the best spot to draw a crowd, but he could always tap the boarded windows with his umbrella to emphasize his points. A handful of stragglers and their children were gathered around him. I joined them. I liked to straggle.

Beanie spoke only English so he barely got across to the immigrants, but much of the time he was beyond the rest of us, too. It didn't matter from our end. We were there for the spectacle. The children were there for the pinwheels he handed out free.

"Only one party can save the human race," he was saying, pumping his yellow umbrella into the air like an enthusiastic tour guide. "It's not the Democratic Party and it's not the Republican. It's the Birthday Party!" he declared high and wide, "and you can be president! Yes, you!" He pointed to us, one by one, then tossed confetti into the air. "I hearby appoint each of you Honorary Presidents of the Birthday Party." He reached out to pat a little girl on the head, but she shrank from his touch. As sweet and ineffectual and ideally suited to his role as community pet as Beanie was, he smelled. He couldn't always attract an audience, but he always had his share of flies.

A trademark cap on his head, Beanie wore a white lab coat covered with hundred-dollar Monopoly bills. The coat was plasticized and a good thing, too, because Beanie didn't just walk in it, he slept in it—in a vacant lot west of downtown—and when the coat got real cruddy he just hosed it down.

He didn't take to water himself.

When the dog days kicked in Beanie smelled like hot plastic, which was an improvement. But we weren't there yet.

". . . get out of that easy chair and exercise your rights! Take your brain out for a walk!" Beanie urged, digging a ball of Silly Putty out of his pocket and bouncing it on the sidewalk. It went out of control, rebounded above our heads. Someone caught the gray matter in midflight and bounced it back. He was so goofy it hurt.

"Declare your independence from the United States of Atrophy! Fight the Farces of the Rich! And while you're at it, give the experts the Bronx cheer. They're only experts at lining their own pockets. They know which way the wind blows." Beanie pointed to his hat, a structured felt number topped by a laminated dollar bill in the guise of a weathervane. "Remember: today is the first day of the rest of your life. Talk back! You can do it! Happy Birthday to you!" he crooned.

Somebody cheered, then everyone laughed. I even managed a woozy smile. It was a bright April morning. A stiff breeze was spinning Beanie's dollar bill around like crazy. It was riveting. Or maybe it was the Seconal.

Beanie wouldn't have been happy to hear this, but it wasn't what he said that moved you, it was the way he said it. There was something childlike about him, beyond the bells and whistles. His skin was as pale and translucent as a newborn's and strangely unmarked by the streets, and when he wasn't speaking, his eyes were round in wonder, his mouth open and lax. Maybe that's why we were all a little protective of Beanie. He looked like he needed a nipple.

Somebody left. Beanie began to hand out the pinwheels before all interest flagged, wagging his finger at the parents. "Don't forget which way the wind blows!"

My neighbor pinched his nose. "How could we?" he said.

All of a sudden Beanie looked down at his feet. "Where was I?" he asked his tennis shoes. The crowd exchanged knowing looks. When Beanie was in form, he was our Mahatma Ghandi, Karl and Harpo Marx all rolled into one. When he wasn't in form, he was on board Spaceship *Enterprise.*

"Scientists," a pleasant woman in a sundress helped Beanie out.

Beanie's head jerked up. "Science! The Science of M&M's—the military and the multinationals. Do we really need a billion-dollar map to our genes when we can't afford walkers for our seniors to cross the street? How about a multibillion-dollar spy-satellite budget so secret even Congress is out of the loop? Do we really need planes that fly by computers and get computer bugs at 10,000 feet?" Beanie paused, too long for a dramatic device. There it was. A wire had crossed. ". . . and get bugs . . . and Bt . . . and Bt till all the butterflies fall from the sky . . ." Then Beanie started to recite facts and figures about soil bacteria, as though summoned by some merciless inner librarian with a bulging catalog he had to plunder if he ever hoped to rally us deadbeats.

His inner librarian had it wrong, though. No one wanted the facts. One by one, people lifted their laundry baskets and grocery bags, rounded up their children and scattered back to their hardscrabble lives. Beanie didn't blink. He was busy flipping through his files. One kid, bigger than the rest and unfettered by a parent, ran up to Beanie and snatched the remaining pinwheels.

This time Beanie reacted. He looked down at his empty pocket, then at the fleeing boy and called out after him, his face screwed with anguish and incomprehension. "Captain Kirk?" he cried.

In short time there were only two of us left, myself and a stray retiree with a fishing rod.

". . . You win, Darwin!"

The fisherman left.

Beanie scratched his head and sat down on the sidewalk where he'd stay till the police would come by or he'd snap out of it on his own.

I picked up his fallen hat and set it back on his head. If only the rest of him could've been as easily arranged. It was sad. He had such a good mind, when it worked, and his heart—well, let's say it was generous to a fault, and leave it at that.

Happy Birthday, Beanie.

A block away, the Jensen Recreation Center was a hulk of an old brick building, three stories of faded glory on the corner of Sunset and Logan, with a resident hotel on top, offices and retail space on the ground floor, and more retail space in the basement where the billiards and bowling alley used to be.

On the roof, a twelve-foot neon bowler was condemned to roll a perfect strike in obscurity, for eternity, because the neon had fizzled long ago and had never been replaced.

Besides the dentista, the pawn shop, my office, and Teresa's beauty parlor, Jensen's was home to an urgent-care health center and a discount center. One-stop shopping. Teeth.

Body. Scalp. You could even get your ashes hauled at Jensen's, upstairs, room 313.

The building breathed survivors. Like Willy, one of its fifty or so residents, who was waiting for me outside my door, below the sign JOE'S WORD: Writer for Hire.

"Hiya, Joe," Willy said, rubbing his hands.

"Morning."

"Kinda late today, aren't ya?"

I got out my keys. "Can you stand back a little?"

"Sorry." Willy stepped aside while I rolled back the gate, then followed me into my office, hat in hand.

I took my time getting to the mail. Sure, it was perverse of me, but it was perversion on a small scale. I opened the blinds, turned on the machines, checked the FAX. Willy stayed glued to my back.

"That was some game last night, huh," he squeaked. "Three and O, bottom of the eighth and the bases loaded?"

Teresa had replenished the stamp supply.

"What did ya think of the fight? That was something, huh. Valdez got six stitches!"

When there was no more avoiding it, I sat down at my desk and got out the letter opener. "Do you mind?" I asked, glancing over my shoulder.

"Sorry," Willy said, stepping back.

I was making it hard on him. He had to crane his neck. I attended to each letter one by one until I got to the end of the pile. "Nope, nothing for you," I said. "Not since the letters that came last week. Which I'll get to today," I promised.

"That's what you said two days ago."

He looked crestfallen, a crestfallen old cock. For a moment I almost felt sorry for him. "I got a new catalog. You interested?"

"A new catalog? You bet! What kind—melting pots? Yeah, let's do it, let's do it now." And Willy was back in the ring, posture upright, every inch of his five-foot-two frame crackling with energy. He passed his hand over his bald spot and the strands of hair he lacquered there.

Willy was my biggest client. I'd started writing for him when I first opened shop three years ago—nothing important, this and that. Over the years, though, the jobs had taken on another dimension, one I couldn't face today before a good ten cups of coffee. I opened my appointment book, a dime-store edition bound in fake cowhide. I told him I'd see him at five and pushed him out the door. Teresa would be gone then. Not that she didn't know what was going on— she'd been working part-time secretarial for me since day one—but I didn't like her around when we went over Willy's file. For his sake. And for mine.

My business card says I'm trilingual: English, Spanish, French. My French was elementary but it looked good on paper and luckily that's where it stood. As for my Spanish, I could talk the talk, but I needed Teresa's help nailing down the written page. With English, at least, I was in my element and in a section of town that could use my help. Still, even there I had no illusions. With my computer, I'd made an investment in technology at Joe's Word that the average resident hadn't. Public writer was just a hook. I was selling my hardware as much as my head.

Apart from Willy, résumés were the bulk of my business. They used to be a snap. Once you'd done the personal statement, they were mostly a question of entering data in the computer, keeping the format tight and pumping out originals on rag. But things were shaking up in the business. All the money was going to dog and pony shows.

All the money . . .

I had a couple of business clients, too. One paid me to write letters to his international investors and send them out by modem. He was Mexican. The other was a Korean who used my office as a mail drop. He'd made up a phony letterhead with Sunset as his address. I'd had to grease the mailman — Joe's Word was on the Logan Street side of the building — but I'd been reimbursed.

What else.

Occasional mailings. A term paper here, a grievance there. Love letters, end-of-love letters. A speech, a leaflet, announcements. You'd name it, I'd write it, no questions asked. I charged by the hour, half a plumber's going rate.

My morning was routine. Somehow I managed to slog through it. Not long after I got rid of Willy, I had to get rid of Ed Hutch. I waved Ed to the client's chair. He sat down as gingerly as if I'd offered a seat in a public toilet. Geez. The place was clean. Teresa and I had given it the once-over after the pigeon flap.

Ed was the president of the Echo Park Merchants Association.

"What can I do for you, Ed?" I asked finally, after a particularly dull exchange of small talk.

"I won't take a second more of your time. I know how busy you must be," he said, without a trace of irony. "I wonder if you'd give me the pleasure of being my guest for lunch today. I've gotten together a few of the boys. We need to discuss this street vendor business, and I thought it might as well be over a couple of bottles of wine. What do you say?"

Hutch was the manager of Les Frères Taix, a restaurant in the heart of Echo Park surrounded by guard dogs and a valet parking lot. It catered to downtown commuters who knew, through experience, they could venture off Glendale a couple of blocks without getting shot.

The "boys" would be the franchisers on Glendale who pulled in the commuter dollars. Maybe Manoukian would be invited. Teresa would not. I said I was busy.

Hutch looked disappointed, then he said he hoped we could make it another time. "I'd hoped for a little solidarity from your end, Joe," he continued. "If they round up enough signatures, we're going to get immigrants here from all over the city—as if we didn't have enough."

I didn't say anything.

"I talked to Al Manoukian this morning," he went on, lowering his voice. "He said he saw you buying corn last night in front of his store." There was a long pause, which would've been silent if it hadn't been for the dental drill next door. "You could get food poisoning, you know. How can you patronize these people?"

"Who else is going to sell me roast corn?" I answered.

He had to admit I had him there.

After I got rid of Hutch, I finished up a résumé. I'd met with Carlos Espinosa earlier in the week. Usually I spent a half hour or so talking with résumé clients, hoping to hear something—anything—that would set them apart. You weren't always successful, but the time wasn't wasted. You noted their character.

And Carlos—well, he was a straight-ahead kind of kid looking for an office job. I'd recommended a classic-type résumé with various extras, but he'd squelched the extras and we'd settled on bare bones. At least he hadn't asked for anything creative. I couldn't afford to have more clients walk out the door.

The rule in these sessions: write down what the client wanted to say. Play up what the employer wanted to hear. That's the way the world turned. Who was I to stand in the way?

Sometimes, though, you had such straight-arrow clients, they had to be coaxed onto the merry-go-round.

"So where did you say you worked before?" I'd asked Carlos.

"I haven't, sir. This will be my first job."

"It will be if you get it," I'd pointed out. "Now where was that job?"

"Beg pardon?"

We'd switched to Carlos' abilities and accomplishments ("I wasn't so hot in high school, but I was a hard worker") and his dreams for the future ("I want a big car that doesn't break down"), and at the end of the interview I'd told him I'd help with his future by giving him a past. It wouldn't be the first time I'd listed Joe's Word as a job reference. I liked Carlos and thought he'd make some employer satisfied.

I'd typed up his facts the other day after he'd left. All that was left now was to write the essay.

Boiling down a life to one page isn't hard when you're nineteen. What's tough is the process of self-examination required in writing a personal statement.

I shifted position in my chair. It was a silly and self-conscious act, but somehow it helped me assume a new voice and identity.

I probed deep inside me, searching for the uniqueness of Carlos Espinosa.

Ever since I was a child I've been fascinated with systems, the way an organization communicates within itself for the purpose of efficiency. It could be something as practical and concrete as the motor of a car, as abstract as the modalities within a religious group, even the manner in which an ethnic group assumes . . .

I hit the erase button and started again. It was no good to oversell.

Ever since I was a child, I've noticed I was different from my family and friends. Whereas others were asking, "What's on TV?" "Who's playing tonight?" and "When are we leaving?" I was fascinated instead by the larger questions of How and, most important: Why. Why a piston connects with an engine at a particular point. Why a priest remains celibate or a nun chooses to serve. Why a Chicano remains soldered to his family despite community pressures to part. Why is what made me tick.

I know now that many questions will remain unanswered, that we don't always know Why, or even How, which is why we have Who, What, Where, and When to divert and occupy. Yet I also know that someone who persists in wondering at life, at the organization of systems and the bonds of family and friends—this someone will always have an open mind and enterprising spirit, qualities which I believe translate readily into the problem-solving skills and creativity which business today needs more than ever to compete.

When you ask yourself "Why Carlos Espinosa?" I believe you'll find your answer here.

It'd do if no one took a hard look, and no one would. I double-checked the spelling and punctuation, and allowed myself a little laugh. Carlos had his How and Why; for me the key was Who. Who was How I paid my rent.

I chucked Carlos in a drawer, arranged the pens on my desk and ducked next door for a coffee break.

Teresa and I had communicating storefronts. It couldn't get more convenient. She always had coffee brewing in one of those machines, and I always went there to drink it.

From the giggles I'd been hearing through the ventilation slat, it looked like this morning I'd be getting mine served with a side of cream.

Three

Hair Today was empty. No customers, no surprise. Just Teresa and her daughter Gloria, who was giving Teresa a hand cleaning up, and Willy in his favorite seat, looking on, swinging his feet.

"Morning, Slim," Gloria said to me.

"Hiya Joe!" Willy called out, as if he hadn't seen me an hour earlier. He joined me at the coffeemaker, poured himself a cup, and carried it back to his seat.

Teresa called after him. "Hey! Your quarter."

Willy slinked back, slid a quarter onto the saucer so that it wouldn't clink. He lowered his eyes as he passed Gloria but he needn't have bothered. Gloria was taking off her latex gloves, one digit at a time, making her move on me.

"I made us a pie," Gloria purred, wedging herself between me and the counter while her mother chewed out Willy over the rising cost of coffee.

I stirred my coffee and smiled back. "I can see that."

"Lemon meringue. The lemons are from our tree. We were waiting for you."

23

"You shouldn't have. I'm going to pass. I . . ."

Gloria reached up and buttoned my lip with her index finger, then she shook her head slowly and sadly at me and drew up closer still, so close I could see the fibers in her T-shirt stretch. "Pass, my ass," she said, caressing the words. "You need to work on your love handles, my boy. How can anyone get a hold of you?" Then she pinched my buns.

I'd gotten used to Gloria's behavior. It was just theater. The important thing was we both knew the terms. We'd spent a damp half hour together a couple of years ago, behind the partition where the washing machine was, but I'd managed to get a grip. What was I going to do with an eighteen-year-old on my hands—and Teresa's youngest daughter, to boot? Gloria had taken my retreat with good humor. In retrospect I'm sure I was just a yardstick for her. I'd told her once I was a fighter pilot in World War II and she'd said that sounded dreamy. I think she'd even believed me. Later that night I'd taken a hard look at myself in the mirror and found, for the first time, hair growing out of my ears. At any event, the washing machine episode was soon salted away, and Gloria moved on in more appropriate directions. She fed her cakes to fraternity boys these days, but she still practiced her moves on me. I didn't mind.

If Teresa disapproved, you'd have never known it.

"So?" Gloria poised a knife above the clouds of eggwhite. "What'll it be: medium-large, large, or humongous?" I told her petite and she made it major and I laid it on a ledge where it couldn't be missed.

The others ate their pie in silence while I drank my caffeine. First Teresa, then Willie gave Gloria the expected thumbs-up. Gloria had been getting thumbs-up since she was ten. Last year, after nine consecutive tries, she'd won first place in a national bake-off contest and had been flown to Miami for the awards ceremony. She was studying English Literature at UCLA, but postgraduate she saw herself Dessert Chef in a fancy restaurant. She already had her toque.

"Somebody got run over yesterday on Glendale," Teresa said, scraping up the last traces of lemon rind. "Hit and run. Near the pet hospital."

"Glendale? Again?" Willy said.

The two of them launched into a review of the lastest robberies, rapes, and mayhems culled from the crime pages of the local freebie.

". . . you know the empty lot next to the car wash? Cordoned off with yellow tape . . ."

I spotted a young woman out on the sidewalk peering through the window at us. "Customer!" I interrupted, and Teresa ran out and grabbed her. Two bits she'd get my piece of pie.

I went for more coffee.

Teresa whisked the woman into a chair, spun her around and moved into high gear. "With your texture of hair and particular bone structure," she told the face in the mirror, molding the air while she talked like an architect at a press conference, "there is only one way to go: you want a body wave for volume," she declared, "under a modified layered bob."

"No I don't. I want to look like Shanna."

"Of course you do! She is so ravishing. But Shanna, she has a very different kind of hair than you, and . . ."

"I want to look like Shanna."

I picked up a hairdo magazine and flipped through the pages. The complete Shanna look cost only eight dollars and could be achieved, according to Teresa, in fifteen minutes — blindfolded — by anyone who'd been toilet trained. Teresa dreamed of customers who would give her carte blanche to create fantasies "like in the fashion shows," but those types lived on another planet. Teresa was lucky to get three customers a day, two of them Shannas. Her only hope — and hope she did, scanning every pilot — was for a new megawatt TV star with a specially charismatic and structured head.

Teresa's husband had died in an industrial accident a while back. The settlement had paid for her kids' education and the down payment on the shop, but the last few years had been a struggle. The neighborhood had gone from bad to worse. Teresa had often said, half in jest, that if it weren't for the paycheck she got from my place, Hair Today would be Gone Tomorrow.

My place. She looked to Joe's Word for security. I started humming the Happy Birthday song. My mind was following its own dotted lines.

Teresa drew me up short. "Hey!" she warned me. "Beanie's rubbing off on you."

"Is there anything left?" Willy quipped.

Gloria piped up. "Did you hear what Beanie said about those gut-type germs? Remember awhile ago, when everyone was getting so sick?"

"You're telling me who's sick?" Teresa said, wrapping a strand of her customer's hair around a brush. She leaned over the Shanna and asked: "Would you care for a piece of pie?"

I handed over my plate.

"Beanie says they're using them in food—in biotech!" Gloria poked her finger in her mouth and pretended to retch.

I yawned and stretched and yawned again, then picked up another hairdo magazine. I should've gone back to work. I should've slept another five hours. I should've voted last November.

I could feel Teresa's eyes on me, could feel her tallying up my office hours and falling short at the bottom line.

One more cup of java and I'd get back to work.

"Why don't you just go intravenous?" Teresa cracked as I finished off the pot.

"You okay?" Gloria asked, her young forehead furrowed.

"I had a white night last night, that's all, no big deal."

"You had a white night?" Willy asked. "Want some uppers? I know where I can get some. Wait a minute—I'll go upstairs and get you some uppers."

Willy looked hurt when I declined his pills.

"There was a robbery at the carnicería," I explained to Gloria. I managed a laugh. "It was botched. Some kids went in through the air shaft and got stuck. The police helicopters circled our hill for two hours. It got a little crazy."

"Did you complain?" Gloria asked.

"Why bother," I said.

Everyone clicked their tongues in sympathy, except for the Shanna who ventured that it was a good thing nonetheless that the helicopters were there to protect us.

"From two guys stuck in an air shaft?" Teresa looked at the woman as though she regretted giving her the piece of pie.

"They're supposed to help. They did a study. I heard it on TV."

"And who funded the study?" Teresa asked the Shanna. The Shanna drew a blank.

I blew into my coffee.

"My neighbor got caught once by a helicopter patrol," Willy said. "He was taking a leak in an empty lot. They trained their lights on him till he tucked in his weenie."

"They're just overpriced flashlights. How much did Beanie say they cost?" Teresa frowned at her lack of memory.

"We should hire one to hover over the mayor's house!" Willy declared in his high squeak.

"You can't do that!" the Shanna exclaimed.

"Of course not," I said, getting up. "No pilot would risk his license." Willie shot a rubber band at me and missed. It landed in the pie plate.

I went over to the sink and rinsed out my cup. Mother Teresa flexing her whip. Hair Today. Gone Tomorrow.

Looking to my place for security.

Four

I checked my wallet when I knocked off at noon and it was where I'd left it: too flat to cover even a lunch tab.

My bank, like the Jensen Building, was one of the original structures in Echo Park. It looked like a vault built for Uncle Scrooge and it was just as tight. The moneymen there had given me loans in the past, a dribble here, a dribble there. The last time the suits had turned off the tap full stop. I hadn't told Teresa yet; she'd only fuss.

I used the robot teller so I wouldn't have to face a live one, then tucked my mad money into my pocket and followed my stomach down Sunset. I didn't feel much like fish soup today or a midnight sandwich either. A block beyond Les Frères Taix and its lot of shiny cars stood the only high-rise in the area. At its adjacent coffee shop, the Brite Spot, you could eat strawberry shortcake and BLTs with parsley and sliced orange trimmings. You could feel right at home in quaint America.

NOW SERVING ESPRESSO AND CAPPUCCINO! a new sign on the door read. Sure. *Va bene.*

I slid onto my stool, ordered the usual from Belinda, nodded to the regulars. The Japanese executive. The two eggheads. The old lady who ordered canned peaches. I recognized the table of Latino businessmen, too, and the cops by the window eating on the cuff. Police were high profile in the neighborhood. Their academy was nearby, their watering hole, the Short Stop, even nearer.

It was my favorite bar, too. What was I going to do—boycott the local with the best beer in town on tap? The cops and I got along. We didn't talk.

Belinda was bringing my order from the kitchen when the front door flew open and a bunch of flyboys spilled in. She laughed and stepped up her pace, but one of them snagged her apron strings and gave her so many twirls that by the time he'd finished, she was breathless and dizzy and the poached egg on my hash was cold.

"Sorry 'bout that," she said to me as she lowered my plate, a smile still squatting her lips. I wondered if she'd ever been upstairs for a spin.

There was a landing pad on the roof of the high-rise for radio and TV choppers. Pilots and cameramen rode the elevators to the Brite Spot for their meals and coffee breaks. I ignored them, too.

It was my habit to read the papers at lunch. I'd find a meaty article, then fold and tuck the section under my plate so it wouldn't disturb my neighbors. Today I waded through the sinkers to an insurance bill and an announcement of a new molecule that would save the human race. After I'd finished with the hash, Belinda came by to ask if I'd like some pie.

I looked up, surprised. I'd been eating at the Brite Spot for three years and had never ordered dessert. "It's fresh today, Joe," she said in a loud voice, laying her hand on mine and giving it a squeeze. That was an even bigger surprise. Belinda had given up on me long ago. We'd never reached the washing machine stage. She reeled off other dessert options, too, one by one, carrying her voice like a bowl of cherries to the booth behind my back.

I looked over my shoulder at the object of her affectations, and there, of all people, among the pilots, was Pete Mathias.

Pete Mathias. I remembered his name straight off. "Hey Pete!" I said.

"Joe!" he exclaimed once he'd placed me. "I'll be damned."

Belinda backed off.

Pete brought his plate and coffee to the counter next to me and slapped me on the back. "I'll be damned," he repeated.

He'd always been big, but he'd put on some padding. It looked like he'd been lifting weights in his spare time. His neck was as thick as his face.

"So you're a professional pilot now?" I asked.

"Yeah, ever since I left the Peace Corps. Which was . . ."

We fixed the date, then exchanged smiles, not knowing where to begin. We didn't like each other.

He had some sun damage to his skin — occupational hazard, I supposed. Mostly you noiced his mustache.

Pete plunged in. "I met my wife on my very first commercial job, ferrying out groups from Puerto Montt, down in Chile. We came back to the States a long time ago, though. What a change, huh? Got two kids now, live in the 'burbs— and I'm flying a Eurocopter 350 B-2."

"Top gun?"

Pete gave me a smug smile, then forked up a wedge of pancakes. "I'm pilot-reporter for the local CBS station," he said when he'd swallowed. "So how about you?" His eyes narrowed. "What're you doing in Echo Park?"

"I'm a public writer—you know, a writer for hire."

"Are you serious?" he said once the words had sunk in.

"Not very," I admitted.

"Here? In Echo Park? How in the hell did you end up doing that?"

"I had trouble finding work after my last job. In accounting," I added.

"Accounting!" He laughed. "My God, Joe—how low can you go?"

I didn't answer. The jobs I could cite. I tell my clients to build a life, but I'd gone the other direction, a slow spiral down. But that was okay. You had to flap to stay on top.

I motioned to Belinda for an espresso. Normally I got my fix at Carmelo's down the street while I thumbed through the Hispanic free press, but I figured I'd make an exception today and keep Pete company.

"I ran across a public writer once, in Paris," I said. "He was operating out of a storefront in a working-class neighborhood. I figured I could do it, and I was right. Why not? I'm a liberal-arts grad." We both laughed. It was a regular laugh fest.

Belinda arrived with my espresso and a pot of house blend for Pete. She hung around behind the counter afterward, checking the ice machine.

"You can't be making decent money from that." Pete shook his head. "Got a wife? Girlfriend? Or are you into boys now—is that why you're laying low?" When I didn't answer he looked me up and down. "It's one thing to live like this—like we all did in our twenties—but what about your future?" This time he didn't wait for my response. "You living in the area, too?"

"Yeah, I got a nice little place. In one of those four-unit bungalow courts."

Pete turned back to his plate suddenly and let out a belly laugh. "You always were a loser," he said. "For the life of me, I never understood what Jenny saw in you."

I tasted my espresso. It was as watery as I'd expected.

"What'd you get an espresso here for?" Pete said, pointing to my cup. "It can't be any good." Then he asked, casual-like, "You and Jenny stick together for long?"

"We got married," I said, holding onto my pause, making Pete eat every second of it, "but it didn't last."

"Is she . . . are you in touch?"

"She remarried right away. She lives in L.A. but we don't see each other. She sends me a Christmas card every year—the same one. HOLIDAY GREETINGS! it says in ten languages. I don't know what's the message."

Pete sipped from his mug, his eyes straight ahead.

I was going back, too. All the way back.

I'd set up an aquaculture program in Honduras, that's

how I'd served. Setting up a market economy in paradise: literally, El Paraiso province. It wasn't easy to farm fish in what turned out to be a surprisingly arid spot, but I'd tried, I'd tried to change the native ways. I believed we were there to do good. And then I'd invested so much of Joe in the Peace Corps. Joe with Jennifer, his sparkling blonde wife. Joe and his fraternity of talented youth. The world was ours.

After a minute we moved on to other memories and other alums. Pete had kept up with some of the guys. They'd mostly become movers and shakers. We talked about the new Peace Corps director and the shift in policy from the Third World to eastern Europe and Russia.

"The average age of volunteers is in the thirties now—in the forties in Russia!" Pete said with a snort. "They're all businessmen and engineers; it's nothing but ties to commerce."

"The CIA is dead?" I joked.

The booth behind our back erupted in whistles. In one fancy maneuver Pete twirled off his stool, clamped his hand on my shoulder and told me he had to take off. We agreed we were likely to see each other again now that he was on the CBS beat.

Five

I stopped by Carmelo's on the way back to the office for another espresso, one with a kick. I needed every drop of it once I was back at my desk in order to face Willy's correspondence.

With a heavy sigh I picked up his mail from the in-box where I'd let it stew for five days. I had no qualms. Nothing was pressing in his affairs unless it was in his pants.

I slit open the first of the two letters.

It was from Dai. It was short.

To the Mr. Will I thought I knew,

I don't know where you get your ideas of Asian women, but you are mistaken! I am not that kind of a girl! You are not a nice man.

Yours never more, Dai Bo Yun

The room was quiet; from outside came the muffled sounds of traffic. I thought of Pete's comment. Sure I had a girl—and more than one. I passed them on to Willy when I was done with them.

I fingered the edge of the letter.

Sweet Dai. Too sweet Dai.

What the hell.

I crumpled the letter into a wad and shot it into the waste-basket. No China Doll? Not to worry. Plenty more where she came from.

Teresa arrived to do the books and billing. She worked at a cardtable I'd squeezed into a corner already squatted by file cabinets. If there were a bad earthquake, she'd be buried by Echo Park trivia.

I watched her for a moment at work. She kept her posture even at her desk. It came to her naturally—that and her hair, which was shocking white and hung like a leaded cur-tain down her back. Sometimes she wore it pulled back with a scarf, that was her sole coquetry. No makeup for her. No curls, no artifice. She was a real aristocrat.

Her shoulders rose and fell as she worked; sighs escaped her with the force of a bellows. When she finished one file, she'd flop it onto the floor before starting on another. There was no space to spare in my place, unless you counted the zone between the top of our heads and the fifteen-foot ceil-ing. That's where the air lived and my heating bill went.

It was dark, too. The only window was placed so high that in the winter, at least, when the light was low, Joe's Word had all the allure of a prison.

I didn't have to kill myself to meet the rent.

The pills were finally wearing off, the static lifting. All that was left was a layer of ground fog.

The sighs rising from behind the cabinets were turning to

groans. Teresa looked back at me once over her shoulder, but I saw her coming and ducked.

The second letter to Willy was from the Philippines. He had a thing for Asian women. Rising suns, he called them. The girl's name didn't click, so I checked her against the master list. Corazon Casalang. Fast response. I'd sent my first letter only three weeks ago. I glanced at her agency pull sheet, then took a closer look at the photo attached.

She was a cutie. A childish, laughing face. Broad nose. Cheekbones. Her pose was demure, hands over Mt. Venus.

Dear Will Brigham [her letter read],

It is delighting to receive your letter. You are a wonderful man that is sensitive and has hair on the body, too. I am so happy that you a writer. I think you must know a lot about Life, because of the terrible suffering you artists go through. You are suffering, no?

I am sensitive, too, but not as a gift of fortune, as you. I am raising to be. All girls in the Philippines are teaching to be thinking of the other, and I am proud to keep that age-old tradition.

You see that I am working in textile design. I find good position since I am hard worker and cheerful and because I am a orphan and learn early on that if you do not go forward, you fall back. You see, I maybe know something about Life, too.

My parents are loosing in a ferry boat when I am three. I have no sisters and no brothers. An uncle in San Francisco is sending money to a neighbor, who raise me. I am going to meet my uncle, but he dieing three years ago. I thank the Lord (because I am Catholic) that I can support myself now, but I

feel big hole to be alone and no family. You know how it is to
be lonely, too, how you write in your letter. But how you can
have love troubles, I don't believe. You are handsome man
in your picture and to be in litterature is to walk on a beach
when the sun falls down and the light is gold and there is
seagulls. I am thinking you not meet the right kind of girls,
because I know if I meet you, I am at your beach. But I not go
forward too fast, or I fall back! What I mean is you and I share
so much. I love children and dogs, too! If I have children of
my own, I stay at home and take care of them and this would
be A-okay to me, because I love also to clean and cook. I
believe woman belong inside the home (except sometimes
the beach) because that is where she finds fillfillment.

I am so happy to know you through your beautiful letter,
Will. I hope to know you more.

Salutations from me, Corazon Casalang

They all said the same thing at first. They thought that's
what we wanted to hear.

Aside from a general understanding of what we were
after, Willy and I had never gone over step-by-step what was
to be said in his letters. Only once, at the beginning, had he
offered any direction. He'd said he wanted me to wing it and
just be myself. I'd been given what Teresa had always hoped
for: carte blanche, dropped in my lap. My lower lap. I
couldn't deny on occasion I found pleasure there.

Though sometimes it made me squirm.

"It's five o'clock, Joe," Teresa said, getting up to go. "I
haven't finished with the books yet. I'll need another hour at
least."

"Two o'clock tomorrow okay?"

She didn't even look at her appointment book. "Okay," she said. Then she paused at the door. "Joe . . ." she began.

" 'Night, Teresa." I shifted position, shuffled paper. When I looked up, she was still there.

She turned around abruptly. The door clicked shut.

I got out Willy's personal stationery and my thick-nibbed fountain pen.

A thick-nibbed fountain pen: in general, that's who I was. A fountain pen because I was sensitive, even sensual in a suppressed sort of way; a thick nib because I was manly, not effeminate. My tone was stiff, slightly pompous at first, but with the passage of time and letters, I warmed up and became more human. The girls liked that. They thought they were having a positive effect on me, it gave them confidence.

Dear Corazon [I began],

You have written a letter that has touched me deep inside. I am so sorry to hear that you've been orphaned at an early age. I know what you mean when you speak of a big hole of loneliness, for I, too, have lost both my parents, plus my only brother who passed away two years ago. If only I had married when I was younger, by now I'd have a family with lots of children. I realize now that this is the real wealth in life, not the material kind that can be weighed, but the kind any man can grasp if he has the courage: the rewards of companionship, the feeling that one is a part of something larger than oneself. I believe in love, I so want to believe! But there's one thing that's troubling me about all this. It has occurred to me, Corazon, that if I'd had a daughter, by now she'd be about your age. Now, I am in the prime of my life and have plenty of vitality left in me in the manly department, but I wonder if someone as young and pretty as you could ever find fullfillment with someone old enough to be your father. I don't mean initially, of course; I mean in the long run.

I hope you don't mind if I speak so frankly, but I think it's best that the subject be broached. I think it would take a woman who is very aware of herself and her sensuality, and perhaps that is asking too much of youth. All I do know is that if I found a woman like this — like you — someone so bright and resilient and so obviously in love with life, I would cherish her and never let her go. I would take her to the heavens in a hot air balloon, to scout our new horizons as far as the eye could see. I would snip long-stem roses from our garden, still heavy with dew, and leave them on the kitchen table for her to place in a crystal vase. When nights grew cold, I would fix a crackling fire, wrap her in my arms and disappear with her into the dancing shadows.

I would make her understand that she is not alone, and that her well of loneliness would never be empty again.

If you think you might be this young lady, I couldn't be more pleased. Of course, it's too early to tell if we are really meant for each other, but I have been seduced by your charming letter and hope to see many more to come. Another photo, too, would be greatly appreciated. Also, one more request. Could you describe yourself a bit? I suppose it's because of my literary bent, but a few words can often make an image take shape, and I would feel so much closer to you, as though you were actually by my side. For example (along these lines): what is your favorite body part?

I must go now. I so hope to hear from you again, Corazon. I just hope you haven't found me too forward.

> Yours truly,
> Will Brigham

Willy had come in while I was finishing up. I'd waved at him to come back later, but he'd ignored me and hung his hat on the rack. He'd been sitting across from me, watching.

I made Xeroxes of all the material, slipped the originals into two folders, flopped them on the desk. I kept the copies for my own files. W for Willy, that's where I kept his girls.

I looked at Willy. Willy looked back.

I pointed to one folder. "This is Corazon Casalang. She's new." I pointed to the other. "This is Dai Bo Yun. She canceled."

I'll say this for Willy: he never put on a front. He shrugged; that was it for Dai, on to the next. "Let's see that new catalog you were talking about," he said, combing his hand over his freckled bald spot, over the scraps of hair he'd tinted bright carrot. He'd done the job himself. Teresa had never called him on it.

There were a dozen bride agencies around. We generally used two of them, one specializing in Russians, the other international in scope. They all had slightly different m.o.s. The new one that had arrived, *International Match*, sent you a free catalog of four hundred desiring brides. You could write up to ten women at a time, but to get their addresses you had to buy a membership. Prices varied. Major credit cards were accepted.

The catalog people suggested their clients visit the girls they thought might be marriage material, but that would've been beyond our budget.

We were corresponding with seven women at the moment—eight, before Dai dropped out—all at varying stages of intimacy. It was complicated to know where you stood emotionally with every girl. Perfect files were mandatory.

Willy leafed through the new catalog. All the women were attractive and educated—they had to be to qualify—but the more stars next to their photograph, the younger they were, and slimmer and sexier. They were allowed to have one child, max. None of the four-stars had children.

"Get a load of this one," Willy said in his squeaky voice, thrusting the catalog in my face. "Page thirty. You like her? Isn't she a dish?"

I didn't answer.

"Which ones do you like, Joe? Check out page thirty-four. What d'ya think? See page sixty?"

He handed me the magazine; I flipped through it dutifully. "You got the cash for a Membership Plus?" I asked. Willy had gone for the three-stars. It was none of my business, I was paid the same either way, but Willy was straying from his usual orbit.

His nod was matter of fact.

Willy used to pitch peanuts at Dodger Stadium. He'd showed me an article written about him once in the *Los Angeles Times*. He'd been a mini-celebrity. He told me he used to do a little betting at the games and had put his winnings in the stock market.

He looked like a peanut, too.

I gave him back the magazine and told him to take it upstairs. "Take your time with it," I advised him. "Consider character as well as charm." But he wouldn't go away.

"You like brunettes, right? Didn't you tell me you like brunettes?" He was all wound up, feet swinging away. I couldn't see them behind the desk, but I could feel the current.

Getting rid of Willy was as easy as getting rid of ants. I finally just took his hat down from the rack. "Time to go, Willy. I'm closing."

Willy still didn't move. He just sat there, swinging his double knits. He had a large and varied wardrobe. He liked to visit the sales ladies at St. Catherine's Thrift, and they liked to make him look sharp.

"Wanna go for a beer, Joe?"

"Nope."

"My treat."

I waved his hat. "Sorry."

He got up, hiked up his bell-bottoms, tucked his catalog and files under his arm. "You were married once, right? Teresa told me you've been married."

He never stopped trying to get close.

I parked his hat on his head and pushed him out the door. I watched him walk off down the street, spring in his step. Five'd get you twenty the only thing Willy had ever pitched women was peanuts.

I was looking forward to bed tonight. I figured a good ten hours of sleep and I could recuperate.

A little exercise beforehand, a little nightcap: these would help to numb the thoughts that wouldn't lie down in my head.

I went home to get my car and returned and parked down by the lake.

There's something sedating about lakeshores, back to the womb, lapping waters and all that. White noise: you could find it even here on the shores of Echo Park Lake though you'd have to get down on your knees to hear it above the sounds of the Glendale traffic. While you were at it, better wear blinkers, too, to edit the pop bottles and beer cans resting in the muck.

The park had been something in its heyday. I'd seen the old postcards with their weeping willows, gents in boaters, ladies with parasols. Even now, if you squared your hands right, you could frame a vision a city father would love. There were still groves of swaying palms, the famous lotus bed, swans gliding on twilight waters through the rosy haze of car exhaust. And at the south end of the lake, rising above the jets of the grandiose water fountain: the mighty skyscrapers of downtown.

I dropped my hands; the cliché fell away.

I took a turn around the lake, then lay down on the grass, hands cupped behind my head.

Lapping waters.

Crab grass. The sting of horseflies. Sand between your toes . . .

Late afternoon. Air heavy with the scent of lake laced with outboard fuel. The dock shimmering hot. Lighter fluid on a breeze from the beach . . .

. . . Yoo-hoo, Joey . . .

Lapping water against canoe hulls, the gulls, the slap of sunfish on the glimmering wet . . .

Yoo-hoo, Joey . . . hoo, Joey. Will you butter the buns? . . . butter the buns? . . . butter the buns?

It was dark when I awoke. I brushed off the grass that clung to my pants and went back to the Boulevard to buy myself some dinner. Afterward I moved on to the Short Stop and bought myself a few drinks.

I had an accident on the way back. I wasn't even thinking about my future. I just slammed into it.

Six

I went straight to the coffee pot. Teresa was there, pouring Mrs. E. a cup. After a perfunctory nod to the assembly, I told Willy I'd take him up on those uppers he'd offered the day before.

"Sure thing, Joe," Willy said, jumping up. "Another white night? More cops and robbers?"

"Something like that. Cops, plus fun and games. I got to touch my nose with my eyes closed, walk a straight line and spell my name backward. I even got home free—praise the Lord," I added, for Mrs. E.'s benefit. "At three A.M."

"You got stopped for drunk driving?" Willy looked thrilled. Mrs. E. looked shocked.

"No, I got stopped by the car I hit. The cops came afterward."

Everyone wanted to know the details, but what was there to tell? My blood alcohol came in under the limit so I wasn't charged with drunk driving, but there was that moving violation and all hell to pay. My insurance would cover the repairs on the other guy's car, but my own car wasn't covered and it was a wreck.

Mrs. E. wanted to know if I was okay, but Teresa's question cut to the bone. "How are you going to pay for the repairs?" she asked, lips crisped.

For a moment the only sound in the room was the clink of my spoon. I turned my back on Teresa. "Thank you so much for your concern, Mrs. Ellroy. The rest of me is okay. It's all in the head."

"I'm so sorry," she said simply. In her eyes I was one of God's children, almost–drunk driver or not.

Mrs. E. had worked at the International Church of the Foursquare Gospel down the block till she retired fifteen years ago. She was very old and very poor. Teresa gave her free permanents.

"Let me know if you need a lift anywhere," Teresa finally grunted.

Willy returned waving a baggie. "My neighbor down the hall," he said, proud of his contacts.

I watched Teresa put the rods on Mrs. E. while I waited for the zing to hit. Teresa had urged Mrs. E. once to style her hair like Aimee Semple McPherson, the founder of Foursquare. But Mrs. E. had said "Oh, no!" with a tremolo, and she was right to put Teresa in her place. She didn't have enough hair to pull it off. Between every rod lay a stretch of pink scalp.

"Want a piece of Strawberry Supreme?" Teresa asked me, holding out a plate as though it were an apology. "Gloria's working on a new shortcake."

"No thanks," I said.

The chit-chat picked up where it'd left off.

"They found the body in the park," Teresa said. "The kids found it, of course. There's no suspects and no motive."

Willy huffed. "And no investigation, either, wanna bet? The police are probably glad—one less transient on the street."

"Maybe it's a jealous husband. Remember the freeway on-ramp lover?"

"The one who sold oranges?"

"That wasn't all he sold."

Mrs. E.'s hand went to her throat. She wore a white detachable collar embroidered on one side with the words: "GRANT ME . . ." and on the other: ". . . SERENITY." There wasn't enough room for the complete credo.

Mrs. E. was proud of her accessory, she said it was a collector's item. You could take it off and wash it when it got dirty, she'd told us, without having to wash the whole dress.

We changed the subject. We all liked Mrs. E. and watched our language around her. But we were just as glad when she left.

When Mrs. E.'s head was ready Teresa helped her over to the dryer. Then Teresa tidied up the shop, sweeping Mrs. E.'s fallen hair into the hair bag, refilling the sugar bowl and whatnot. There was one piece left of the strawberry thing. "Any takers? No?" Teresa tossed the crumbs to the pigeons lined up waiting on the street.

I gave Teresa a dark look, which must've triggered something. She suddenly stared at me as though she'd never seen me before. I nearly shrank into my seat—the pills must've taken hold.

"You need a haircut, Joe!" she announced, coming after

me. "A new one, a new style. I can give your face an illusion of breadth. Why not look your best? Anyway, we need new photos of you for the girls," she added in justification, but it didn't wash. It wasn't my face the girls were after, and then I've always found it reassuring in the mornings to recognize myself in the mirror.

I negotiated a shampoo/massage and hold the blow.

I leaned back in Teresa's reclining chair and eased into the neck mold. Warm water rained down on my head, and for a sweet moment I managed to forget my buzzing brain and the men at the garage gauging at this very instant the extent of my financial ruin.

Teresa squeezed out shampoo from a bottle and started in at the temples. "More gray hair, Joe."

"Thanks, Teresa."

I wondered if Teresa had ever sat in this chair and seen Hair Today from the customers' point of view. The donkey piñata with its belly full of grime, the fallen sconces, the rusted air vents. Teresa had made an effort to dress up the place. Garlands of Christmas lights draped the walls, and celebrity heads from magazine spreads were tacked to a bulletin board and changed religiously once a week. But it was like Willy doing somersaults in order to cover his bald spot.

Behind the partition the washing machine shook, the cassette deck had a warble, and the hair dryer a buzz. When Teresa had set up shop five years ago, she'd had a canary, too. It'd loved the commotion and sang all day on its perch. But it had died.

Hair Today. Teresa's coal mine.

When Teresa was finished, she made me step outside and pose for her instant camera. She said I was a knockout in the wet look, and it was true we needed new snapshots for the brides. Willy tagged along and watched while I tried to look soulful.

I returned to the coffee machine and poured myself another cup. I'd get to my desk right after this.

"Customer! Paying customer!" Willy cried out, getting into position.

I took a glance at her as I headed back to my seat. What was the story here—had she gotten lost? She was dark and light and skin and bones. She looked like an ad for unfiltered cigarettes. It's not that there weren't birds like her in Echo Park, but they stayed on the hilltops with their own kind. They didn't mix with scavengers.

I picked up a dog-eared magazine.

"How You Get Back at Men: A Personality Test." I flipped to page 52. I enjoyed guessing who filled out the blanks in these sorts of things. You couldn't tell from the handwriting; it was a scratch of numbers and scores. Was Teresa or Gloria "The Ballbuster"? Was Mrs. E. "The Mater Dolorosa"? It seemed too pat. I thought of the parade of women who'd passed through Hair Today. Under the hair dryer they'd learned who they were.

Teresa and the customer were discussing the haircut. Teresa wanted the girl to grow her hair out, which would mean multiple visits and money in the till through the whole transition.

"How to Get a Bonus from Your Boss."

"Think of what you could do with updated long hair! It's feminine and graceful, yet still so sophisticated. You could wear a chignon at night—like Grace Kelly!"

"I don't want to look like Grace Kelly," the girl said. "I want to look . . ."

". . . like Shanna, yeah I know," Teresa said, breaking in with an axe.

"Who's Shanna?" the other said, surprised. "I want to look like Jean Seberg."

I looked up over the ledge of my magazine.

Teresa turned to me. "Who's Jean Seberg?"

I gave a short laugh. "You going to go all the way?" I asked the girl. My magazine was turned to "Are Blondes Better in Bed?"

But Teresa lost out on the peroxide job. The girl wanted to keep her hair black, raven black against that creamy skin. She just wanted Seberg's haircut. She pulled out a photo of the actress and showed it to Teresa.

I took a closer look at her when she was getting her hair washed. Mid-thirties. Black jeans, white T-shirt. And under the T-shirt, a set of breasts . . .

I got up, poured another cup of coffee, took the same route back.

. . . real ones. You could tell by the way they lay.

"Would you like some coffee?" Teresa asked the girl once they were settled again before the mirror. There was real warmth to Teresa's voice. She'd never done a Seberg before.

Teresa was blocking my view of the mirror, beginning to snip around the nape of the girl's neck, when another shadow passed before the door. It was Grand Central this morning. Some guy carrying a clipboard came in, but before he'd uttered two words he was cut short by a helicopter buzzing low and fast. The windows shook. Under the hairdryer Mrs. E. looked terrified, till we pointed to the sky and eased her mind. It wasn't an earthquake this time.

The guy with the clipboard cleared his throat when the chopper finally gave him the floor. We turned our attention to him. We always gave people the time of day. That was all we had to give.

"I'm with the Associacion de Vendadores Ambulantes."

Teresa leaned over the girl, remeasured her marks. "Does this look right? Or you want it shorter."

". . . We need to get enough signatures on the petition to set up a vending zone."

"I thought that went through already," Willy said.

"It only allowed them to set up. And now the police are cracking down. We need your help."

The cut was so short her ears stuck out, but I approved of the back. Her hair dovetailed down to the base of her neck.

The organizer circulated his petition. There was a block of gray matter at the top. Mrs. E. got the clipboard first. She got out her bifocals.

The haircut was over, but the girl didn't leave. I supposed she was waiting to sign the clipboard. Teresa swept the fallen mass of her hair into the canvas hair bag.

"What're you going to do with that?" the girl asked.

I spoke for Teresa. "She sells it to Mrs. K's Chicken Feed, you know the shack on Sunset?" Teresa looked pissed, like I was giving away a trade secret. "When you put human hair into mole holes in the garden, it scares the moles away."

The girl looked at the hair bag, then at Teresa. "Do I get a cut?" she asked. Teresa gave the girl's arm a whack.

It was Willy's turn with the petition.

Teresa warned me she had a manicure scheduled next. I got up to leave. Manicures gave me the vapors. "Don't forget Mrs. E.," I warned Teresa. We'd forgotten Mrs. E. once, left her under the dryer. She couldn't lift the hood on her own.

"Wait! I'm almost finished," Willy called out, whipping off his signature and holding out the clipboard for me.

I turned away. "I don't sign petitions," I said, ignoring the blast of air conditioning on my back from Willy's and Teresa's direction.

I don't know what the girl thought.

As I closed the door, our eyes met.

Seven

I got going on the phone. First I called Hank's Garage for a ballpark and it was as I'd expected: a line drive to the gut and we weren't even talking cosmetics. We pretended to haggle over the price of used replacement parts, but I had no leverage.

Then I called the insurance company to learn how much my rates would rise, starting with the next premium, which was due in three weeks.

I wondered if I could ask . . . nah, it wouldn't be right. I sat back in my seat and stared at the ceiling.

If today was the first day of the rest of my life, I needed a boost and hell if it was going to come from one of Willy's little pills. There was that letter in today's mail. I'd been looking at it from the corner of my eye while I'd been wading through the muck. It was from Moscow. Natasha from Moscow. I could be with her now.

We'd been corresponding with Natasha for almost two years. She wasn't like the others. She'd never enclosed a personal photograph, had never wondered when Mr. Will would come for a visit. She worked as a translator in a foreign service, that much I knew from the agency pull sheet and from her crack English. That was her day job. At night she came home to me.

Fuck repair bills. Fuck insurance clerks. Fuck Mother Teresa and creative résumés.

I reached for the letter opener and slit open the envelope. I could feel the sap in me rising. She was that kind of a girl.

I have just come in from the fields.

That's how she started. No greetings, no nothing. That would've spoiled it.

I have just come in from the fields. I have been all day poking and digging in fields half frozen, half thawed, of mud. The light that was white and veiled this morning has turned a dirty yellow. We will soon have snow and it will be welcome on a land so bare and exposed. Only a trace of last week's snow remains, unspent, in the dark of the furrows.

I range my boots in the mudroom and hang my coat on the heavy hook Grandfather forged and beat of metal, but I cannot so easily slip out of the mud. It is clay, wet and heavy. It covers my shins and has splashed under my skirts. I try to wipe it off, but it clings and slides between my cold fingers like wet grease. Objectively the mud is something to admire. The heads of industry and their foremen should kneel before me and feel for themselves. They could learn a thing or two about lubricants for the workings of their machines.

But the industrialists and their foremen, they won't come. I am alone. Ten days now I am alone.

I start a fire with willow twigs and shop paper at first, next
branches thick as a man's fist. When the flames begin to lick,
I feed logs from the pile one by one. The heat edges into the
room; my clothes drop to the floor. With a warm wet dripping
rag I slowly lift the mud from my legs. Drip, rinse and wring.
Drip, rinse and wring again. The cloth is rough against my
skin, but it feels good. It warms me up, makes me feel alive. I
rub myself all over, it feels so good, then slip on a clean sleeping gown. It, too, is homespun and stiff. I am naked beneath
and tingle from the rough.

I have not yet lit the lamps and it is dark inside. Only the
flare of the fire lights the far reaches of the room, the pantry,
the door to the bedroom, the root cellar. From the direction
of the barn comes the plaint of a cow.

I sit down to the roots, pulling the pail onto the table,
heavy with its load. Turnips, parsnips, rutabagas. They smell
of earth and mud. I take a fat parsnip, peel back its surface,
unrobe the firm, pale flesh beneath. It is something, this flesh
of the earth that begins as a small insignificant seed and swells
and swells, growing long and large, probing deeper, ever deeper
into the dark earth until it shoots up its stalk and scatters its
seed to the wind.

Across the dark the cows are calling. The sound is muffled.
I get up, scratch a patch of frost from the window. Snow has
started to fall. It is falling fast. It is so quiet, save for the call
of the cows. It is as though a bell jar has come down upon us.

I reach for another parsnip. The clock above the hearth
records the moments with a dry, wooden beat. It is a presence
in the room. The only one. Ten days now. Ten days I am alone.
I look at the parsnip in my hand, turn it over slowly, set it
down on the oilcloth. The old oilcloth with its clusters of

cherries scrubbed dull over the years. I peel a rutabaga, then a turnip and then another parsnip still, and when I've finished I place them in the pot where the beans and the bones lie waiting. Ten days alone.

From the barn another call. This time I must go.

In the courtyard the snow is falling fast and wet. It melts as it strikes my face.

The cows look up in tandem, in silence, as the barn door creaks slowly open. Their breath rises in vapor clouds above their heads: Lena, Marishka and Ninotchka. They shift their weight; the stall walls creak from the contact of their flanks. The barn smells of hay and animal.

Ninotchka: it is she who has called, my favorite, the one who knows me. She is wanting her salt.

"Ninotchka," I say to her, fondling her ears. She tosses her head. She is the mother of Lena and Marishka. She is gentle, but she is wanting her salt.

And I am ready to give it to her. I move close, lift my skirts and open my legs. I take the sack of salt from the nearby ledge, pour out a handful and drop the grains onto my fur. It sifts down, I can feel its drift. I step closer. Ninotchka's nuzzle touches me first. Lena and Marishka watch the two of us, detached, as they might watch fish jump in the pond behind the barn or a fox steal across a dry pasture. They lower their heads from time to time for another mouthful of hay. That is not how I feel. It is not hay I am wanting. I jerk from Ninotchka's contact, her nose is so cold. As she starts to lick, I reach for the stall wall to steady myself. Her tongue is as rough as a man's whiskers who has not shaved for three days, but her moves are deliberate and slow. She is in no hurry, she is a cow, she will lick as long as it tastes good. I direct her tongue and her rough kisses with small movements of my hips, for it is she that is tethered and I who am in control. The more she licks the more juices I have to give. Lick and lick and lick. Until, with one last move, a spasm shudders through my body and I pull back and drop to the floor.

After some minutes I get up, shake the straw from my cloak and quietly shut the barn door behind me, on the warmth that I have known.

A wind has come up. I double bolt the door.

I throb long into the evening.

The letter paper was coarse. I rubbed my hand across it. It was one thing for Willy to say I could write the way I felt. But my job was to get the brides to open up for him, and my feelings had nothing to do with it. What was needed was a suppleness of style and a sensitivity to each girl's needs. Basically, I wrote whatever it took.

For Natasha I got out my ballpoint, got on my horse, and whipped up the purple prose.

I am coming from town. I am three days early and one day late, for the storm has set me back. The last few kilometers the snow has glazed my brow and beard, but I am driven and will not be stopped. I lash the mare, push through the wet dark. I can see you at the end of the road, you and your flanks white as the banks of snow that pass. I rush headlong into the hurling night, towards the sweet, walled valley that I aim to plow.

Yia! Yia! I cry to the mare, Get on! but the wind sucks the words from my mouth and throws them into the streaming void. Two more rutty kilometers to go, and you at the end of the road, you and your sweet bush I will part and sunder.

Vlovnik's lamp is on my left, blurred and dim through the swirl of snow. One more kilometer, one more kilometer to go. The mare and I can smell it now: home, the manger, your quim. There is no stopping either of us. We hold the memory of our own madeleines.

Our own lamp is not lit, you are not expecting me. A glow through the kitchen window marks the remnants of a fire. I jump off the mare. She is wet with snow and the froth of sweat. I rub her heaving sides with rapid strokes, for my member has risen with the ride and the thought of you, and I cannot wait till I am at your side.

I step into the mudroom. Clods of snow drop off my boots onto the bare planks. You will be hearing me now. You will be heavy from sleep, heavy and warm as eiderdown, and full of soft folds that will plump to my touch.

I throw my coat onto the hook, cross the hearth in two strides and open the bedroom door.

It is a moment before my eyes adjust to the dark. The light of the fire behind me casts my shadow over the bed. You are awake, on your side, facing me. I move to you, so close I can feel the heat rise from your sleeping gown. I bend towards the nape of your neck, rub my lips against your skin, suck your skin. I am so hungry for the flesh of you—I will eat you, eat you and your fleshy folds where they swell and turn red and wide-open. I reach under your robes, slide my hand tense and slow up your strong thighs towards your thicket, my member pulsing tight. I am full of fluids and

—but what is this?

So is your snatch.

I step back.

You have not had time to be wet. How can you be wet so

soon? It has been only a moment since I have awakened you. My voice is low and quiet when I speak.

"You have been with the cows again," I say.

It is not a question. You do not reply.

Now I cry out. "You like animals?" I am wild. I grab you by your shoulders, throw off your gown and go down on your bush, inhaling the smell of straw, mud, the odor of animal and sharp cheese. I lift up my head and begin to slide rough over you. I pull myself up, higher, higher still, till the weight of my body has fully straddled you and my cock is flush with your face.

"You like animal?" I cry out, frenzied. "I'll give you animal then!" I take my member in my hand and whip your mouth till your lips are bruised and full. Your panting breath on my red hot tip — I am ready to explode. "I'll give you animal then, and not some pussy cow lick! Milk me!" I press myself in and out. "Milk me! Harder! Harder! You're not milking!" I cry. Then I pull myself out of your mouth one last time and shift my plunges into your hole below, your sweet, gaping wet hole, again and again and again, till at last I spurt my seed into your deep and roll off you, breathless, onto the bed.

We are talking, some time later, about this and that — the price of goods, the calico I brought back from town — when Vlovnik appears at our bedroom door, his massive build filling the frame.

You stare at me wildly, hopelessly. "You didn't lock the door?"

Vlovnik, filling the frame. Swaying, stinking drunk.

I laid down the pen, got the keys from behind the door, and went down the back hall to the toilet.

Carlos Espinosa was in my office when I got back. He was leaning over my desk, sack of oranges dangling from one hand, reading my letter to Natasha. I crossed the room in two strides, picked up the letter and stuck it in a drawer. He stared at me. I didn't say anything. I looked at my watch, pulled out Willy's chit, marked my time.

Carlos finally found his voice. "I'm here to pick up my résumé," he said. Then he paused again. "I . . . I was wanting to pay you. Only thing is, I can't pay you today."

"Why's that?"

"My transmission is out and I need to get it fixed. How'm I gonna get to job interviews with no wheels?"

"How're you going to get to job interviews with no résumé?"

"Couldn't I pay you when I get the job? See, here's how it is: I'm broke. I know it's not much, but in the meanwhile . . ." He held up the sack of oranges.

What the hell, the work had been done. I gave Carlos the résumé, a resigned pat on the back and pushed him out the door. It gave me a certain satisfaction to know I'd sussed him out right. He had a bright future ahead of him in business. He knew about spying on desktops, and he'd already learned how to float.

I settled down at my desk again and tackled my in-box. The high point of the first day of the rest of my life was over—what goes up must come down—but the day still lay before me and the amphetamines were pushing from behind.

I started in on a letter I'd put off twice already. My client, Mrs. Bing, wanted her son's high school marks improved and didn't want to bungle her chances with a letter to the principal fraught with dicey grammar and logic. She wanted to attribute Jimmy's failure to Seasonal Adjustment Disorder, but I'd persuaded her to go with a broken home instead. We'd had a laugh together coming up with the details. And I'd enjoy giving the old saw a tweak: Nature or nurture? Neither. Jimmy would be shaped by my pen.

Willy stopped by while I was working. We chatted a few minutes about the girls from *International Match*, but Willy hadn't come to a decision yet.

I wrapped up the letter soon after he left, ending with a heartfelt plea that even moved me. Before slipping the note into the envelope, I dipped my finger into a glass of water, shook a couple of drops over the stationery and quickly blotted the spots. Things were looking up. I figured I'd just earned enough for a new car headlight.

And then more money walked in the door. Another kid.

They were all kids these days.

"I wanna work in the music industry," this one said, pulling up the chair. He threw a wad of green on my desk. In the silence that followed you could hear it uncrinkle.

"Why not go for Hollywood?" I asked.

He waved me away as if I were a gnat. "I'll need to be marketed. I'm low on credentials, but that didn't stop David Geffen from reaching the top, right? Am I right?"

"Yeah."

"A little spit, a little polish—you buy me?"

"I get the drift."

"I want something really riot—something that expresses the uniqueness of me."

Spike hairdo, fringed leather jacket, studded rubber bracelet. Man overboard. "I don't think I can help you there. I'm sorry," I said, getting up to show him the door. "I'm a sober man."

"Well, no wonder you're so uptight!" the kid said. He reached into his hip pocket and pulled out a pint. "Here—take a hit on me. Cut loose, man. Have fun!"

I thought of the state of my car at Hank's garage. I looked at the money on the desk and the pint bottle in his hand.

Creative résumés.

I took the bottle, a swig and a leap.

I wondered how much I could charge.

"I was thinking along the lines of a multimedia pitch."

"Got a Swiss bank account?"

"I've got the Bank of Mom. She'll do anything to get me a job." He paused. "Would that really be expensive?" He paused again. "Well, okay, we can scratch that. Anyway, I wouldn't want to come across too . . ." he searched for the word.

"No, wouldn't want that," I replied. I sighed, got out a scratchpad and took down his vitals. He lived on one of the hills, an okay address. He had an okay education, too, though he thought it could be improved. He wondered aloud about the Ivy League, but I told him not to push it and we settled for as is. Then I went through my string of stock questions.

Any skills? Know how to operate the latest software? Can you crunch numbers? Speak a foreign language?

Things like that, plus others more personal and probing.

"Where do you see yourself in ten years?" I probed.

The kid thought for a moment, absently rubbing the ring in his nose. "Ten years? . . . Yeah . . . Yeah, I can see it. It's eleven at night; me and a babe are cruising down Sunset in my Mercedes convertible, looking for a pre-concert pizza."

"I meant in terms of the industry."

"That *is* the industry," he said, tsking at my ignorance. "Where you been—under a rock? Here, have another hit, man. What you really need is some good weed." He had to explain it to me: "I'll be one of those scouts paid to check out raw talent. The blonde at my side is my personal assistant."

"All right," I said. I drew a significant doodle on my pad. "Now, one last question . . ."

"Riff."

"Riff. Just as a wild card, mind you: What would you want to do if you didn't get into the music industry?"

You didn't always get a revealing answer for that question, but you always clocked time, and I was charging by the hour. My résumé clients always pondered the question as though it were important.

"Take your time," I said. Riff's forehead pleated like an accordion.

"I would be a piano tuner," he said at last, with conviction.

I looked at him with sudden interest. "Oh yeah? I thought you said you didn't play any instrument."

"I don't. I have a tin ear. But I like the idea. I like the idea of searching for perfect pitch. Like the Dalai Lama says."

"Well," I said, picking up the money that had sat on the

table during the interview. "I suppose you can always sell drugs if I can't get you a job." I counted the money. It wasn't much.

"That's just a deposit," Riff said, noting my expression. "I'll pay the rest when the résumé's ready, but don't give me a bill, okay? Let's keep this cash. I'm going to Ensenada to put in some party time—you're only young once, right? So there's no rush. Shall we say three weeks?"

We shook on it and off he went, leaving behind in the palm of my hand a couple of professionally rolled joints.

I put them down on the table next to the sack of oranges.

Eight

At closing time I cleared my desk, locked up the shop and set out for home.

I sniffed the air; it smelled like rain. I gazed out over the turnip fields. The light that was white and veiled this morning had turned a dirty yellow.

By the time I'd reached the ridge on the other side of Glendale, I was walking through the first mists of a drizzle. That's when I heard the explosion and saw the fireball—a big ball of red-orange flames—erupting above the trees no more than a half-dozen blocks away, followed by a thick plume of black smoke.

I won't say I actually ran to what looked to me like a helicopter crash, but my sack of oranges was slapping against my thigh and I managed to work up a sideache. I wasn't alone. The whole neighborhood was on the run.

The firefighters had just arrived, shouting directions, hauling hoses, getting lines on various fronts. A couple of parked cars were engulfed in flames, and a brush fire, ignited from debris hurtled into the shallow canyon, had gotten out of hand. Residents were doing what they could to help, stamping out fires here and there.

The chopper was pulverized, a mass of ashes at the foot of a dead end. One thing I wasn't about to forget was the lingering smell of burnt fuel and flesh.

The media arrived and organized. Vans with satellite dishes, reporters with stern faces. Up in the sky, Pete and his media fleet circled. Police scoped the situation from up above, too, while their colleagues below took the lay of the land. For a half-second I thought about Riff's joints in my hip pocket, but of course that was absurd, they were too busy doing crowd control. The locals weren't happy with the turn of events.

The cops were interviewing witnesses, too.

"It was hovering over the fence where the kids hang out," a woman in curlers was telling an officer. "You're always bothering us so I wasn't watching, but I heard a funny sound and I ran out and looked up. The helicopter was real low . . . the pilot was looking down at me . . . straight at me . . ." She started kneading the metal fence in front of her. "Then it started spinning and then it crashed. It felt like an earthquake."

The cop told her to take a tranquilizer.

I noticed for the first time that a resident had been hurt. He was sitting up. It didn't look too serious, but he may have been in shock. The paramedics wouldn't let the media near.

Although the major fires now seemed under control, the cars were still smoldering and sporadic flare-ups in the darkening street continued to contribute to a generalized sense of

hell. The mood of a bunch of women had turned from bad
to ugly. They were screaming at the police above the whop
of chopper blades. "Our kids could've been killed!" they
shouted in English, Spanish, Chinese.

A chicana suddenly broke from her sisters, ran over to a
TV crew filming nearby—Pete's station, KCBS—and thrust
herself in the camera's face. "Police state!" she cried. The
reporter asked her a few questions before resuming her
commentary.

After we'd all milled about awhile, the first drops of rain
fell, and I went home, put the oranges in the icebox, and
turned on the news.

". . . mechanical difficulties less than an hour ago in the
Echo Park area."

I switched to KCBS, might as well check out Pete's work.
And there it was, the shot from SkyCam 2 recorded earlier—
the zoom on the ashes, the pull-back on the charred cars—
while a talking head gave the names of the dead and the
bystander being treated for superficial wounds and shock.

It was said that five boys had been spotted at the dead end
prior to the crash. The chopper may have been investigating
their activities.

Then the coverage cut to what looked like a schoolyard
and a reporter wearing a T-shirt emblazoned with the
acronym DARE. Behind her were a clutch of children
dressed in the same T-shirt. "In what appears to be an ironic
twist," the reporter intoned, "Officers Ames and Campbell
had just come from the nearby Mayberry elementary school
where they'd performed a flyby as part of a special DARE

graduation ceremony. The children are aware of the terrible accident, of course, and officials say tomorrow they'll receive special counseling. Our city's finest were positive role models to these kids—in an area of town that could use them. They were heroes because they DARED to give more than lip service in the war against drugs. Every day, they DARED to fight crime. Sadly, today they put their lives on the line and lost, and now their families will be dressed in black. . . . Back to you, Ed."

The interview with the chicana had been left on the editing floor. In fact, there was no sign of the local protests at all. Instead we'd been treated to a promo for DARE and the LAPD, and left with the innuendo that the five kids had been dealing drugs.

Drug dealers, I snorted. Human interest.

I couldn't eat my dinner. At eleven I switched on the news again for an update.

"We're Looking Out for You!" the logo read.

". . . with a startling new development in this evening's police helicopter crash—only two blocks from the Glendale Boulevard artery during the height of rush hour. We've just learned that gunshots had been fired at the aircraft moments before it dropped. It has also been confirmed that the police were descending at the time to look into what has been described as "gang activity." These gunshots, Larry, will be something the LAPD and the National Transportation Safety Board will be looking into as they investigate the probable cause of the crash. Surprisingly, there may not have been a mechanical failure at all."

"This'll be tough to investigate."

"Yes, it will, Larry. Police officers have been unsuccessful so far in their attempts to question the suspects, because the young men scattered at the time of the crash and have not been seen since. The LAPD has asked local residents for their help in providing information related to the shooting and to the whereabouts of the young men—but there, too, they are coming up short."

"It's the same old problem, isn't it, Margo."

"Yes, it is, Larry, one of the more frustrating aspects of a police investigation. Should neighbors inform on neighbors? If they do the right thing, could it come at the cost of their own lives? What exactly is the psychological toll on communities caught in the crossfire? Investigative reporter Barry Brandon has been asking himself questions like these, and— starting tomorrow at eleven and continuing every night this week—we'll be bringing you an exclusive KCBS-TV special report, "To Snitch or Not to Snitch?""

"Finally, Larry, one last development related to the helicopter crash. Manuel Hernandez, the bystander hurt on the ground, has been unable to furnish his identity papers. He could turn out to be an illegal."

"Guess he wouldn't file a lawsuit then?"

Margo raised her eyebrow in a shared moment with the TV audience, then pointed out that the officers of the Air Support Division were passing the hat to pay for his hospital bill.

That did it. "To Snitch or Not to Snitch?"

I took my third beer and a Simenon to bed.

The rain that'd been pussy-footing all evening now pelted

the windowpane. It was late in the season for a storm. I slid into the cold sheets and waited for the warmth, and when that didn't come, I slipped on a pair of socks.

I listened for a moment to the gurgle in the gutters. With an effort I managed to push out of my head—at least for a while—all thoughts of the crash and coverage. But that only made room for others.

I couldn't afford to give Riff the money back. What in the world could I dream up? I must've been crazy to take the assignment. I wasn't visual.

But then I still had three weeks.

Nine

Beanie was handing out balloons, giving the locals a lift.

His crowds had increased threefold since he'd dropped his other causes to concentrate on the helicopter crash. Emotions were still running high among the immigrants, gringos, bananas, and coconuts.

"This sky is my sky, this sky is your sky . . ." Beanie sang, Woodie Guthrie style, "this sky was made for me and you." Then he urged, "If you think the rich and powerful have stolen our sky, stand up and be counted! Join the Birthday Party! Happy Birthday to you . . ou . . ou . ."

My neighbor passed me a balloon. "Happy Birthday!" he said. I said "Happy Birthday" back, but I drew the line at tying the string around my wrist.

Beanie raised his slender fist. He was in a rational mode today. "That helicopter was on routine patrol. It wasn't on a mission to protect people and property, it hadn't even been dispatched to cover a call. It was on routine patrol. Every day—nineteen hours a day—the LAPD is up there just twiddling their blades, out looking for trouble. Like 'misfit' cars that don't 'belong' to a neighborhood, people running who aren't wearing jogging outfits, people just hanging out, like those boys in the canyon last week. We know their routine, all right. They hover, they chop and pop the air, they train a spotlight on their suspicions.

"Ever heard of the Fourth Amendment? This is invasion of privacy, abuse of power—not only harassing anyone who doesn't stay inside, but turning our homes and neighborhoods into combat zones . . ."

A squad car pulled up across the street. Two officers eased themselves out and ambled over to the Salvadorean corn vendor as though they'd just gotten the urge to chomp a cob. They towered over the woman, their backs turned to me. I couldn't see her face, only her skirts and her children, wide-eyed, clinging to them.

It was way early for lunch.

". . . In 1989 the Supreme Court upheld police use of choppers at 400 feet. 'No undue noise,' the justices said. Now how many of you think these justices have ever lived in the inner city, have ever been subjected to helicopters hovering and terrible earsplitting din?"

She'd gotten a ticket all right. Her face was all knots. The cops, on the other hand, were all smiles. They were on a roll. They got lucky with a jaywalker right in front of their eyes. They jaywalked to our side of the street to nab him.

A balloon burst and everyone jumped, but it wasn't gunfire and so we all laughed. Beanie's momentum was shot, and he had to wind it up again.

"Look! Up in the sky!" he cried. "It's a bird! It's a plane! No! It's a chopper!"

The cops were now leaning against a nearby car, casual-like, working on their tans.

"The fact is that the LAPD has no policy on how low choppers can go during a search. If you want to complain about a chopper hovering over your house, you have to prove it was a hazard. It's hard to prove. How hard? What percent of complaints result in infractions of FAA Code 91.119? We don't know. Because the FAA keeps no statistics on complaints. They're not tracked!"

The crowd stirred with real interest.

"You can prove it was a hazard if it falls on your head. You win! You lose! But of course helicopters are supposed to be safe. Just like nuclear power plants: safe till it's too late.

"It's a wonder there aren't more accidents. There's more helicopters in L.A. than any city in the world except Tokyo. We've got nineteen airports and 150 heliports. The LAPD alone has seventeen copters, including A Stars worth $1 million and the new Bell 407s at $1.6 million a pop. And it takes a lot of cash to keep them up in the air. On *routine* patrol.

"How about the whirlybirds from the sheriff, fire, and city departments, plus the military and all those news stations, too, chasing the action so they can sell more toothpaste tubes. Then there's the commercial chopper business and all their clients: commuters, tourists, rich residents with a whim— like the Westside honcho who has his masseur flown in."

Beanie pointed to his dollar bill. "Wanna guess which way the wind blows? How about in the heavens with the $400,000 chopper Cardinal Mahony rides. Godspeed to the cardinal! Wouldn't want him to mingle with his flock!"

The cops, deep in conversation, slid their sunglasses back on their noses.

I wasn't the only one with one eye over his shoulder.

"You'd think with all that traffic there'd be close monitoring, right? Wrong! There are no minimum altitudes except near airports, no mandatory routes, and no monitoring of traffic." Beanie paused to let the facts sink in. I'd never seen him so lucid and focused. *Star Trek* was light-years away.

"And if you want to complain about the noise—just the noise!—who do you think you have to call? The LAPD, of course. The LAPD Noise Abatement Unit."

The two officers cleared their throats and began to stroll in our direction.

"We'd be better off if we were prairie dogs in Yosemite or lizards on Maui's Haleakala Crater. We've got laws to protect the native species there. What about us? Can't we be treated with the same respect we give a rodent?"

"Can't we . . ." Beanie hesitated. He was staring behind my shoulder. He started again. "Can't we . . ."

The crowd parted. The cops stepped through the breach. They stopped inches short of Beanie and pointed to the confetti at his feet. "This yours?" they asked.

One of the officers got out the ticket book. Beanie looked down at the sidewalk. So did the crowd. Then they glared at the cops and slouched away.

The officers stood with their legs apart.

"Hi," I said to one of them. I recognized him from the Short Stop.

"Bye," I said.

Everything had shot up two feet after last week's rain, including the weeds that sprouted through the sidewalk in front of Joe's Word. It was true. I'd noticed. It was springtime.

I sighed and bent over. If you didn't get rid of them, they'd lift the cement. Maybe I should've let them be. That way they'd cover the graffiti.

I didn't notice at first the package propped outside my door.

It wasn't a bomb, it was from Mrs. Bing. A card tucked under the ribbon read "Thanks ever so much! Jimmy's grade got changed to a C!" Under the waxed paper was a three-layer chocolate cake. She'd included forks and napkins.

I lugged it over to Hair Today. "My treat this morning!" I called out jovially as I nudged aside the mugs on the counter to make room for the plate.

"You bake it yourself?"

I turned around at the unfamiliar voice. It was the girl. "Well if it isn't Jean Seberg," I said.

"She's getting a trim," Teresa told me from the corner. She was sloshing her combs in detergent. "Her name's Clio. This is Joe."

"Enchanted."

"Likewise."

Willy came by in time for the cake. Teresa had a slice, too. The girl and I didn't eat; we weighed each other in the mirror.

"Anyone watch the news last night?" Teresa asked.

"The cop funeral?" Willy said. "Yeah, I saw it. There was nothing about us in the recap. Nothing at all."

"We don't exist," Teresa groused, tearing into another hunk of cake. "This isn't as good as Gloria's," she remarked.

"The chopper should've crashed on the Glendale commuters. Then you would've seen something."

"There was more coverage of the schoolkids."

"The ones from the DARE graduation ceremony?"

"What kind of ceremony was that anyway?" the girl spoke. "Having a helicopter buzz over your head."

"Graduation to real life," I said.

"They don't need a ceremony for that, they get it every night."

"It's not surprising it was shot at," Teresa declared. "I'm not saying it was right or anything, but you keep flying those things too low and someone's going to explode."

"Did they let those boys go yet?"

"Yeah, they didn't have any evidence."

"Remember the kids that shot at that helicopter awhile back?" Willy said. "Remember? When they were spraying us with malathion?"

"Which time?"

"They weren't gunshots," I said. "They were bottle rockets."

"Whatever. It didn't stop the spraying, did it?"

"No it didn't."

There was a moment of silence.

"Oh well," Teresa said with a sigh. She finished off the last of her cake and returned to the girl, taking a few final snips before removing her cape with a flourish and whisking her down with a hand broom. She did a thorough job.

There were those shoulders again.

"Thanks," the girl said. She pulled out her wallet and handed Teresa a bill.

Teresa waved it away. She turned to me. "Joe . . ." she said, voice dangling. I didn't like the sound of it. "Clio and I got to talking, about this and that," she went on. "And you know what? She's an artist."

"I'm not an artist."

"She says she works freelance. What d'ya think? Couldn't she maybe help us out on those résumés—you know, the flashy ones?" Teresa gave me a look, and it was one of those ant things.

I took a sip of my coffee.

Teresa held the whisk broom like a club.

"Well," the girl said, after a long moment, getting up. "Thanks again. It's been a great cut."

I got up, too. "Can't hurt to talk," I said to the girl. "You free now?"

She said, "Now is good."

Willy's legs were swinging.

I showed her to my office and shut the door tight behind us, both the door and the air vent. I stuck my head back a fraction of a second later and caught Teresa frowning. "Manicure fumes," I said, flapping the air. Then I shut her out again.

The girl stood in the middle of the room.

"So," I said, going behind my desk. "Did Teresa give you a run-down of what I'm all about?"

"Not really," she said. She started taking in the office, scanning the walls. "She said you were a public writer," she added over her shoulder.

"She got it right."

I stood behind my chair, too aware of too many machines in too small a space. And this girl with a dancer's body moving through it. I still hadn't had a close look at her face, but she had other landmarks.

She turned around suddenly; I raised my eyes from where they'd been grazing. "I thought they only had that sort of thing in the Third World," she said.

"You've seen where we are? But it's not just immigrants who need help. I get all kinds. You'd be surprised."

"Got a diploma?"

I wasn't sure what she meant. "Actually, there is a school for public writers — in France. But I didn't attend."

She nodded as if that were the right answer. A second later she asked, "What's that noise?"

"Sounds like a root canal," I guessed.

She laughed.

I pressed against the back of the chair. Springtime.

She sat down. I did, too.

"So what's the job exactly?" she asked.

"Résumés, like Teresa said. Ideas and visuals for what's called 'creative' résumés. It's a new gimmick. Even if I liked your style I wouldn't be able to offer much money and I wouldn't be able to offer much work."

"I don't have a résumé," she smiled at me, a touch defiant.

I smiled back. "It doesn't matter. We'll make it informal.

You could tell me, for instance, what makes you think you're qualified."

"What makes you think I want the job?"

I cocked an eyebrow. "Then why are you here?"

I'll be damned if she didn't cock me back. "I've worked off and on in design houses," she said finally, once our eyebrows had settled down. "Mostly off, mostly illustration, mostly at Perkins/Slater and GraphiCo." She looked at me closely to see if the names registered. They didn't. "The last two years I've freelanced. I'm best at black and white. Pencil, pen, charcoal. I've been known to do a wash," she said. She waited out the silence. She didn't offer color.

"I need to know the people I work with," I said at last.

"I can imagine. We should meet again. You'll want to see my book."

"How about tonight?" It flew out. "You like baseball?" I added.

"Is this personal? Or personnel?"

"I'd say . . ." I said, and my jaw did a little shift, ". . . leave your book behind."

She said she liked baseball and then we were on, just like that.

After she left, I paced. But it was done, it was a date.

I hitched up my pants.

I wondered how far she would go.

The rest of the day was tough sledding; my mind wasn't on my work. Willy had finally settled on pages 32 and 66 of *International Match*. We'd gotten the girls' addresses in no

time flat through the catalog's phone sales department. I
needed to get off the introductory letters.

I spread the agency pictures on the desk, not that it mattered in terms of what I wrote. Willy and I had decided long
ago to re-use the first letter I'd ever written, since it had gotten
results. Why mess with success? It was fast and it was easy—
although it still had to be copied each time in longhand.

Once, in an effort to economize, I'd tried typing letters
into the computer and printing out the text, but we'd had
no response at all. It seemed it was my pen that oozed
personality.

Both of Willy's choices were Chinese. To compensate for
the loss of Dai, I supposed. One of them had a little daughter.

Dear Meelok,
    I hope you'll excuse me if this letter seems stiff . . . hairy,
too, but I'm no ape . . . in the literary field . . . a classic-type
garden in front . . . two halves that meet, two pulses that beat
by airmail . . .
                                    Will Brigham

You had to be careful when you copied. When your mind
wasn't on it, you could drop key words.

Then I worked on a gripe.

Gripe letters were a bore, but they were also bread and
butter—especially the ones to officials, because they never
ended. Most of my gripe clients came to me out of exasperation and fatigue. Sap, that's what they wanted from me, and
if I couldn't always raise it, I was good for a certain dogged

quality. Anyway, sap was overrated. The rules of the game, the right syntax, precise vocabulary: that was what counted. Most important of all was what was not said, and the tone of what remained. It was here that I performed my greatest service to my clients. I was cool, measured. It was none of my business. I was just a hired pen.

Aldo Missoni had written five letters to the Community Inspection Division of the L.A. Department of Building and Safety, plus two more to his city council representative before he'd given up and come to me. He'd had no new response in two months, and when I'd reviewed a copy of his last letter, I could see why. The telltale zip code, the grammar mistakes, the handwriting—in pencil, on cheap note-paper—all spelled disenfranchised. But his real error was calling the seat of power an assembly of assholes. No wonder he'd wound up in the round file.

He'd laid it all out for me earlier, including the rusted car parts, the mutilated topiary, the battery acid, and the three A.M. pickups. I'd listened, taken notes. I'd even gone over to his place one afternoon when he'd said the coast was clear.

My work, on occasion, required me to stretch. Sometimes I was a counselor, sometimes a psychiatrist. That day I was a dick.

I could see right off he had a point as well as a problem. For authorities, out of sight was out of mind—what you call "blind justice"—and you couldn't get more invisible than the 1000 block of Terrace View, a cul-de-sac butting up to a freeway sound wall. It was the perfect spot for a stolen car ring.

Aldo lived in a sagging bungalow two houses up. There was never a question of moving—it was the house he and his wife had shared for forty-two years. And the topiaries that'd kept him occupied since his wife's death were as firmly rooted in his lot as his heart.

He told me all he wanted was peace.

I held a powwow with him at the scene. I made it brief, speaking up above the traffic, telling him what he could expect. Dead leaves swirled above our heads, blasted by the passing big rigs. There were dust devils, too. They seemed at home in the place.

That was last week. Yesterday I'd made a few phone calls and gone downtown, and bingo: I found there'd been a violation of the California Vehicle Code. A whole new way to get nowhere.

I sat down before the blinking cursor. The writing for this sort of work comes easy enough. You use two or three words when one would do, and latinates would do just fine.

Detective Bill Ramsey
Los Angeles Police Department, Rampart Division
2710 W. Temple Street
Los Angeles, California 90026

Re: illegal car repair business, 1000 block Terrace View

Dear Sergeant Ramsey:

Since early last year, a group of men have been using the above-mentioned city street as a locale for commercial car repair and other clandestine operations. As a consequence, a continual stream of strangers park their cars in front of my house and leave them in the care of these "entrepreneurs," who, during the day, rehaul engines and strip parts (tossing them into my property), and, at night, confer in hushed tones under the lamplight.

More than once I have witnessed cars loaded onto a truck at three in the morning.

In anybody's book, this is dubious behavior. In the vehicle code book, it is also illegal:

Please see State of California Vehicle Code Ch. VIII, Div. N., Sec. 80.73.1, attached.

I threw in a few more details and ended with a call to action and a two-page account of the consequences of the affair on my property, my finances, and my health. I affixed a dollar amount.

In one last futile gest, I made a copy of the vehicle code and the letter itself to send to Councilwoman Hasfeld of the 13th District, apprising her of the new tack I was taking and apologizing for my prior conduct. I blamed my medication.

At lunch I ran into Pete again.

"Hey," I said, lifting my hand in greeting as I passed by his table. "Saw your work on TV last week."

He got up and followed me to the counter.

"The chopper crash? Yeah, we got pretty busy up there. Belinda, can you bring me another cup of coffee here? Thanks, hon."

I ordered the usual.

Pete turned back to me. "It was quite a scene. Too many of us chasing too little and trying to stay out of the way of the cops."

"Too little?"

"Yeah," Pete laughed. "KCAL even turned their microwave on us to try and steal our picture, but we didn't have anything to steal. There was no action to speak of—besides a puny fire—and the chopper itself was just ashes. It's hard to get personal with a pile of ashes. I couldn't even get my cameraman a tight shot of the Hernandez guy."

Pete had the hide of an armadillo. "That's what counts?" I asked.

"I'm a professional voyeur, boy, I'm paid to titillate. Give me crime and a freeway chase any day. Now that's entertainment. Action sells." Pete laughed again. "Even when you get the wrong car."

"Next crash we'll try to arrange for more wounded on the ground."

"*Walking* wounded," he smirked. "Action news, remember?"

"It would've been nice to hear some context in your report. Helicopter volume, frequency of crashes: things like that."

"What a snore. That's not in our interest."

" 'We're Looking Out for You?' "

"We're looking out for our stockholders first, then our advertisers. Human interest, yes, but public service? *Controversy?*" He preened his mustache. "Natural disasters are the best—too bad they don't happen every day."

"What happens when nothing happens?"

"Something's always happening in L.A., and in between the news and traffic reports I shuttle execs around, work for the studios, deliver kidneys to hospitals for transplants . . .

My work's never dull. It's no desk job," he added, throwing a jab at me.

"You deliver organs? For CBS?"

"I don't work directly for KCBS; I work for a helicopter service. We're leased out to local TV and radio stations on a more or less exclusive basis. In between the news we pick up other work."

Belinda came by with our orders. "Here you are, boys. Let me know if you want anything else."

Pete gave her a broad wink. She ate it up.

"I see you're drinking regular coffee now," Pete said, pointing to my mug. "Got smart, huh?"

"Yeah. Thanks for setting me straight."

"That's what old friends are for."

We passed a moment without speaking.

"Joe?"

"Yeah?"

". . . Forget it. Never mind."

I looked with longing at my folded newspaper. He didn't show any signs of leaving. "Any inside buzz on the crash?"

"Too early yet."

"It must've given you pause," I said, toying with my parsley.

"Naw," Pete boasted. "I've been shot at before—during the riots. Reminded me of 'Nam. And my chopper's got the power to get out of situations, know what I mean? It's a sweet piece of machine. I'm not saying there aren't hazards out there, but you don't get a job like mine without having the skills and the mindset to push a chopper to its limits. It can get tricky. We're flying under the see-and-be-seen rule of the air. You've got to monitor air traffic control frequencies and scan the sky at the same time. Downtown is hell. All those mirrored buildings and all the traffic. You can get scared by your own reflection." He sipped from his mug. Beads of coffee hung from his mustache. "There's a few thousand electrical pylons out there, too. And the wind, and the night flying . . ." He took another sip. "Nearly every pilot has a tale."

Belinda swung by again. "Can I interest either of you in a piece of pie?"

"Not for me, hon. You have a piece, Joe, you could use it. You look like a toothpick."

Belinda tried to press more coffee on Pete, but he held his hand over the top of his mug. He smiled up at her. "You know I can't be taking a pit stop at 1,000 feet . . ."

When he left he executed another spin off his stool, but this time something went wrong. He blanched and reached for the small of his back. He stiffened when he saw my concern. "Occupational hazard," he said, recovering his bluster. "The cockpit's cramped. Lots of vibrations." He gave me a poke in the ribs.

It was a good hour before I got over his vibes. Pete didn't need a pit stop up in the sky. He was peeing on us nonstop.

The end of the day was still a long way off. I thought about Clio while I was sharpening my pencils for the afternoon stretch. I took my time and did a good job. If there was one thing I disliked, it was dull pencils.

Guzman's financials: that was one I could whip off.

It'd been a good quarter. Orders were up, labor costs were down. It looked like I might even consider expanding, the horizon looked so fine. I kept my report vague but tight. Then I pulled up my new graphics software and got buzzing with the numbers Guzman had supplied. In the end I had a document that looked every inch important. Even plausible.

I was pretty proud of myself. Feeling my oats.

I looked up at the clock. A half hour to go. One last appointment and I was out of here.

I got up, locked the door, flipped over the cardboard with the four silly clocks.

One half hour, and counting.

And counting.

He was late. He was going to make me late to pick up the girl. I pulled his file and the bank envelope from my lower desk drawer, the one I always kept locked. Even Teresa wasn't in on this one.

At 6:15 I finally heard the knock. Delicate, tentative, like wind flapping my sign against the door.

I ushered him in. "Hi, Beanie," I said. "How you been?"

Ten

"Sorry I'm late," Beanie said, putting his weathervane down on my desk.

"I'm afraid I'm going to have to leave soon; I've got a rendezvous. Do you think you'll be long?"

"I won't be long."

"Is it true what you said about the prairie dogs in Yosemite?"

Beanie's eyes turned fluid. I took that for a yes. After a moment the mist cleared. "I want to make a check," he said. "How's my balance?"

I gave Beanie a hand with his downtown bank account; that was where the annuities from his trust were sent. "Same as it was three months ago," I laughed. "Plus oodles more in interest." Beanie looked at me as a possum might look at the headlights of an approaching car. "Three months ago," I repeated. "That was the last one. The Echo Park swimming pool? Remember?"

"Oh, yes," he said. "The children." His face was luminous in the gloom of the office. It seemed unrelated to his frail

and knobby body. After another silence he said, "Would you please make the check to the order of the Los Angeles County Public Library? $100,000. One stipulation: that it be spent exclusively on books—printed matter, not electronic, and no books on computer technology, either. Specify 50 percent fiction, 50 percent first-time authors."

The dollar on Beanie's cap slowly rotated out of the corner of my eye. It was distracting. I'd left the door open to cut the smell and it had caught a current. "It'll take me awhile to work out the wording. $100,000, right? Anonymous?"

"Yes. There's no rush, take your time."

"Some proxy stuff came in. Want to take a look?"

"No," he said as he always did. He signed his monthly check and got up. "I won't keep you any longer. I'm sorry I'm late. I know how important the evenings are to people who work."

I laid my hand on his shoulder. It was sticky. "How's your health, Beanie?"

"I'm fine. Thanks for your concern." He started for the door. The flies followed.

"Hey!" I called out. "Don't forget your cash." I got the money from the envelope and made sure he pinned it to the backside of his inside coat pocket, next to the piece of paper with my phone number and address.

We shook hands and I released him back to the street.

Eleven

She was wearing a skirt with a slit.

We took my car, which was more or less repaired, but we parked on Sunset and walked to the gates. Why pay parking fees?

She'd agreed.

I learned a few things about her as we passed the line of cars inching toward the stadium. Like she only looked like a dancer when she stood still. She walked like a lumberjack. But that was okay, she kept up the pace and that was important because we were late. The grid of lights above the stands was starting to outdazzle the twilight.

"Pretty, isn't it?" I stopped for a moment and indicated the view, showing Clio my sensitive side. I was a little breathless from the uphill rise or else it was the car exhaust. At the base of the hill, already in shadow, hundreds of palms rose above the ground mists and roofs of aging bungalows.

"Could use more green," Clio remarked. Her voice, cool and clear, cut through the rumble of a passing Budweiser blimp.

We reached our seats just as the first strains of the national anthem were being massaged. Everyone in the stands rose to their feet. I looked at Clio. Clio looked at me.

"Care for a bite to eat?" I asked.

"Now is good," she nodded and we walked back to the concession stand, leaving the land of the free to the crowd.

Clio was carrying the hot dogs to our seats when she tripped, but she only lost the pickles.

A baseball game is a nice neutral terrain to get to know a stranger. You don't have to force conversation. There's organ music in the background, you're dining out . . .We took a swig of our beers and sank into our Dodger Dogs and joined the thousands of other jaws working out. Everyone was chewing at something—even the players, although afterward they got to spit.

"Salt peanuts! Salt peanuts!" a Willy clone cried.

After the crowd had finished their snacks, they cradled their babies and discussed the weather and their no-good bosses at work. Some of us watched the game.

". . . Fouled away! That's two and two to Wright . . ."

Some kid in our section had the play-by-play on the radio and was treating us to the blast.

I settled back in my seat. I loved the shimmer of a baseball game. The lights were so bright, everything was so luminous, you'd think you were in one of those tunnels that led to God.

Clio was good company. We mostly talked baseball. She knew the ropes and seemed to enjoy herself. She was physical about it. She was up, she was down. She was up, she was down. Yet she sat out the wave.

"It's silly, I guess, but I don't like to be a part of something that's so programmed. I'd rather be a hole in the wave. I like voids," she added with a laugh.

"Oh?" I laughed, too.

". . . Vincent Spado, batting .265 this season," the announcer bellowed, "with an RBI of . . . and that's a HIT! a big hit! Punched deep into right field! It looks like . . . no . . ."

Clio followed the play; I covered the infield. I'd only had a good look at her breasts when she was on her back at Teresa's. Now I had them standing up—and standing up, to all appearances, without the aid of a bra.

". . . and Todd Bright makes the catch and that's two away . . ."

I asked Clio if she wanted another bad beer, and when I returned with our refills, I brushed my leg up against hers and kept it there.

They say there's an earthquake fault under Dodger Stadium. A thrust fault.

In the third inning a swarm of gnats descended on the stadium. They got so thick you could eat them, or drink them in your beer. Some people left, and you could hardly blame them. The Dodgers were already trailing 7–2.

Others shrugged at the bugs. C'est la vie, they said in eight languages.

Clio was the c'est la vie type; nonetheless, it seemed like a good opportunity to step up to the plate. I swung my arm around the back of her seat, unfolded the hood of her windbreaker and adjusted it over her head. "Wouldn't want to mess up your new hairdo," I said. I'd come prepared, too. We peered out at each other from under our wraps, blinking away the gnats. The organ ripped through a rendition of "When You Wish Upon a Star," and there was a whole lot of wishing going on.

It was on account of the bugs the guy didn't see what hit him till it was too late.

"Foul ball!" shrieked the radio announcer. "Foul ball, back to the stands!" Most of the people in our section jumped to their feet, peering through the gauze of gnats, arms upstretched, hoping to make the big catch. But the victim, poor bugger, had his eyes on his Dodger Dog when the ball hit. He fell like a sack of potatoes. There was a scramble for the ball while those nearby slapped his face and shouted for security. We could see him from where we stood. He came around in a minute, but he looked dazed.

It was someone in our row who chanted it first. "Sue! Sue!" he called. Soon our whole section was crying out loud, and then—what d'ya know—the cry got picked up by the neighboring stands, and the stands beyond that and the bleachers beyond that and then before you could say Jack-be-nimble, the wave had formed and the whole stadium was rolling on its feet, bellowing, "Sue! Sue!"

In the background, you could hear the announcer's perplexed squeak: "What was that? Did you get that, Vin?"

The crowd was pumped. It was an event.

I turned to Clio. "Could I interest you in going for a real beer?"

We raced down the steps, through the tunnels and corridors. The stadium was quaking with pounding feet.

We laughed all the way to the Short Stop. We couldn't shake the blimp, though. It shadowed us as we tripped down Stadium Way, a novelty moon with a pesky drone.

"You took me to a cop bar?"

I didn't know how she could tell; they weren't wearing uniforms or anything. Maybe she'd seen the bullet display. "It's a sports bar," I maintained.

"Serving cops. And cop groupies."

"We're here for the beer," I declared, a little defensively. "Let's belly up."

But she wanted to check the display cases first, the county coroner's badge, the joke posters. "Dial 911—Make a Cop Come." There was baseball memorabilia, too, although she was right. It was beside the point.

I steered her away from the stronger stuff.

We found a couple of stools at the bar between two groups of giants drinking green liquid.

"In honor of a visiting bobby," the bartender explained, throwing a rag over his shoulder.

We ordered our pale ale and didn't press. Clio tried to pay but I wouldn't let her. Are you kidding? In a cop bar? "Thanks anyway," I said, sliding my hand down her back. It was bony.

Sly on the juke box. Staple Singers. Dire Straits. Yet time after time it was Frank Sinatra that surfaced. Everyone wanted it "My Way."

" 'Comme d'Habitude,' " I sang along at one point. I figured a Jean Seberg would appreciate knowing Sinatra had done a cover of the original French. But she didn't hear me, or else she didn't appreciate it. Maybe she was a faux Seberg. I excused myself and went to the men's room.

When I got back, my seat was taken by a barrel-chested hunk in a paint-splattered T-shirt. He and Clio were laughing like old friends.

"Joe," Clio said, turning to me, "I'd like you to meet an old friend of mine, Boris. Imagine meeting him here!"

"Great beer here, huh." Boris pointed to his mug so's I could understand.

"He's a sculptor. He works with rusted car parts," Clio added.

"I'm working on ennui," he told me with a wink.

"Let me know if you need a supply."

"Pardon?"

"We've got to move to the back room, Clio," I said abruptly. "Sorry about that," I told Mr. Ennui. "I've put a marker on the pool table."

I left them to say their good-byes and went to the back room and waited. My beer tasted sour. I slapped my glass down; foam spilled over the lip. Couldn't they stick to the formula?

I put a quarter on the pool table.

"He's got a loft downtown," Clio told me when she arrived. I didn't know what she expected me to add. I didn't answer. I took her to a table where we could keep an eye on the game.

I didn't say anything for a bit. I studied the players. Clio remarked on the decor. It was as though we'd walked into a waterfront café interpreted by the set designer of a Doris Day film. White trellises, white tables, white planters filled with plastic shrubs—plus fishnet dotted with chiffon sea urchins.

There were a number of cop groupies in this room. They were dressed like bait.

"The serious pool is played in the back room," I told Clio. "The Veterans of Foreign War Womens Pool Association meets here, too, because they feel safe."

"We're in a space warp," Clio remarked.

"Relax and enjoy it," I said, my hand grazing her shoulder. I got up. One of the wonderbreads had motioned me to rack up.

"You a sharp tuna?" he asked.

"Only when I want to play with my lady friend," I joked, and proceeded to whip the pants off him. It felt good.

Clio wanted to do the crack, don't ask me why. I rubbed my stick in the chalk and watched her moves. She knew how to play but wasn't good.

"So tell me about your freelance work," I said conversationally. "What've you been up to?"

She knocked the white ball into the pocket. She made a face. "We're back to that again?"

"Just getting to know you. You thought you were already in the bag?" I retrieved the ball, set up my shot and missed.

Clio didn't answer right away. She took her time getting her sights on her next shot but she missed hers, too. She went back to her beer and took a fast pull. Too fast. This beer had a head.

"I do dogs," she said at last, licking the foam off her lips.

I came to her side with a napkin. "You missed a spot. Permit me?"

"Go ahead. I do dachshunds, golden retrievers, poodles, you name it. I do portraits in black and white."

I couldn't find any more froth, but it wasn't from lack of trying. "From photographs or live?" I asked.

"Kind of a combination."

"Hey!" Someone called out from behind us as he put a quarter on the table. "You shooting pool or what?"

I stepped back to the table, shot and missed.

The guy looked at us with contempt and returned to the bar.

"You have to spend time with the dogs to find their special nature," Clio said as she studied the angles for her next turn. She hit a ball in the pocket and allowed herself a small smile. "Some dogs don't have any character so you have to put a twinkle in their eye, otherwise the owners won't pay. The bigger the twinkle, the happier the client. You can give them a hangdog look, too. That's popular."

She seemed relieved to get the dogs off her chest, but I think they were still on her mind. As she bent over her next shot her elbows stuck out and so did her rear; at the last minute, she jerked her elbow and missed.

She wanted petting.

I put three balls away in a row, but I didn't want to finish too quick. I tried a crazy bank shot and missed.

Clio got back into position again, and again it was all wrong. I came to her side, pressed in her elbow and laid a hand on her tush. "There," I said. "That's better."

"What I really like to draw is flowers," she said.

"And flowers don't sell?" I asked, looking down at her rump.

"Not *my* flowers."

The guy came back and drummed his fingers loudly on a nearby tabletop.

Clio shot and missed. She glared at the guy.

"Can't take the heat, stay out of the kitchen," he said so we could hear.

I cleaned up then, snapping the eight ball in the pocket. I told the guy to go play with himself. Clio and I retired to the banquettes and finished off our beer where it was dark. Under the table our knees touched.

"Why didn't you go back to those design firms? They must pay good money."

"I hated it. Anyway, it's been seven years since I worked there. I wouldn't fit in anymore."

"Seven? I thought you said you've only been freelancing the last two."

"Are we still in the interview?"

I shrugged. "You draw dogs, I write résumés. It's professional: I see a void, I want to fill it."

"You can't live with a void?"

I smiled and waited.

"I was supported," Clio said. She picked up a seashell and began to play with it. Her hands were fine and slender and ivory—like the rest of her, I imagined. I imagined some more, but I was cut off. "It was great in some respects. I drew flowers every day and got to build up my specs. I submitted them everywhere. I still do from time to time, when I have the courage." Her smile was faint. "When he went back to Germany, I had to get work somehow. I went to the dogs," she laughed. Her laugh, too, was modest.

"He was German?"

"Yes. In the Hollywood Foreign Press."

"Got to see a lot of movies?"

"Yeah."

"Miss the screenings?"

"Yeah." Her hand stroked the seashell.

In the parking lot I pulled her into the shadows and up against the wall.

I stepped back, cleared my throat. My voice still came out like cornhusk.

"What d'ya say to a little coffee back at my place?"

I think she was moved. Her chest was moving.

"I'll throw in a mineral water," I whispered as I dived back.

Ten minutes later I was going into the kitchen to get us a couple of beers.

"So what kind of name is Clio?" I asked.

She stayed in the living room. "It's an award. I was named after an advertising award. My parents were bohos and they liked the way it rang."

"Were?"

"Are."

I peeked around the corner. She was looking at walls again. She was thinking: nothing personal.

When I got back she had shifted focus and was trying to

read me through my bookcase. "What's so great about Simenon?" she asked.

"Unpleasant characters. Atmosphere," I replied, handing her a beer. "Why don't you take off that jacket and stay awhile," I said. If she were hoping for a literary debate she'd rung the wrong number, and so had I. But she let it drop, along with her jacket.

This was what I wanted to see: that little cardigan sweater with buttons like dewdrops.

She pointed to the wall. "Where are the photos of family and friends?"

"I don't have any friends. And not much of a family."

"Never married?"

"Am I the one applying for the job?" I joked. I sat down on the arm of a chair and motioned to her. "Let's see that haircut of yours," I said, pulling her close and twirling her around. I drew my fingers through her short thick locks. There was a spot that didn't sit right. "What's this?" I asked.

"A cowlick. It's not Teresa's fault," she said over her shoulder. "So were you married then?"

"Yeah, I was married. Long ago."

I slipped my hands around her waist and pulled her closer still. A cowlick. Go figure. I brushed my lips down the slope of her neck. Salty. I licked again, and the more I licked, the more I wanted to lick, and then I began to suck. It was all in the skin, that's where it was. It was in the skin that lust was born.

Rub a dub dub, three men in a tub—and nothing happened?

She turned around. Her mouth was parted. "What went wrong?"

Jesus Christ. I drew a deep breath. "Is this a condition?" I asked, trying to keep it light.

She didn't answer.

"I beat her till she bled."

"You unpleasant character," she laughed, but her laugh had an undertow. She was waiting, all right, but I made her wait the length of a slow, thick kiss. In the meanwhile I began a digital search under her skirt.

"We were in the Peace Corps together," I said finally. "We split over ideology. I couldn't teach aquaculture anymore."

She was wet.

"Fish?" she gasped.

"I lost my beliefs. My wife held on."

"How sad."

I pulled my hand out of playland and started in on those buttons. It was as I thought: she was bare underneath. "It was just as well," I continued. "That way she didn't have to face the shame when I got caught embezzling."

This time it was Clio who drew the sharp breath. Maybe my hands were cold. "Happy?" I said.

"Yes," she replied and bent down to rub my neck. "I've never slept with an embezzler before."

". . . that you know of."

She fumbled with my belt buckle. "Did you . . . go to jail?"

"It was white-collar crime."

"What'd you do with the money? Give it to the poor?"

"I bought a new car. It got repossessed."

I got up, pulled her panties down and wedged her against the wall. But it only worked like that in the movies. We decided to relocate and I was grateful for the pause. My cock was getting a whiff of real pussy for a change and it was out of my control. When we got together again — on the bed this time — I tried to keep it slow. I tried to think about molecules and insurance bill amendments, I even conjured up Ed Hutch, but it was hard what with Clio nuzzling my nipples and me working the sweet below. It wasn't long before it was too late. I smothered myself one last time in her coal pussy and shot myself in her void.

"Sorry 'bout that," I said a moment later, when I rolled off.

"It's all right," she replied.

Twelve

The street was quiet. Where were the niños and the men tinkering under their cars? Where were the wives and the babies and the smell of onions cooking? The surroundings felt darker, more subdued, as though more than two lives had been snuffed.

I walked to where the street stopped in a ring of scorched pavement.

The wooden fence that'd marked the end of the road was a fragment of its former self. It looked like the locals had finished off what the chopper had begun—carting off in the dark of night free charcoal and firewood.

I dropped to my knees. The forensic technician, looking for the hidden details, the missing presence, the telltale dried blot of blood. Who? What? With what? Why? How?

I picked up a handful of dirt and dust, watched it sift through my fingers. Scraps of metal and electrical wiring. No sign of metal casings.

"My chopper's got the power to get out of situations," Pete had said. "Know what I mean?"

The wind stirred, carrying the scent of ash.

Know what I mean?

I heard a sound. A lady in a nearby yard was calling me. "Find anything?" she said as I came up.

"No." I gave an embarrassed laugh. "I don't know why I did that."

"I'm still picking up bits of metal myself," she said. She had a Slavic accent. "The police combed through my yard twice, but they left the stuff they weren't interested in."

"You're lucky your house didn't burn down."

"You're telling me. I was outside when it happened. I was terrified. Pieces of metal skidded up to my feet. Nicked one of my roses." She showed me the damage to the bush.

"Did you hear the gunshots?"

"No I didn't. But those helicopters make so much noise. You live around here?"

"Yeah."

"You're not the only one who's come back. I guess we'll forget eventually. The media was wrong about those kids, though," she said almost absently. "They're not bad boys. They hang out there 'cause they don't have money to go to the malls."

"They're not doing drugs?"

"Not unless you consider cigarettes drugs," she said with a rueful smile. "Would you like some lemons? My tree's overloaded. You'd be doing me a favor."

Thirteen

"And this is Greg with his wife and children. He's my youngest." A middle-aged doughboy, in uniform, stared defiantly at the camera. He was holding onto his brood as though they might escape him. Mrs. E. waited for my reaction.

"Un-huh," I said. I passed the snapshot to Willy.

"They ever visit you?" Teresa asked Mrs. E.

"They have their own lives to lead," she answered, groping for the right tone. She found it on her collar. "They get depressed when they visit me. You need to be optimistic to get ahead."

"Family," Clio said.

"Quite a family," Willy seconded, passing the photo back.

Clio was in Teresa's swivel seat again, back for another trim. That was the thing about a Seberg, I was finding out. It was high maintenance.

"You still got that picture, kiddo?" Teresa asked.

Clio rummaged through her purse and pulled out the tattered photograph. What the hell. She carried it around with her?

Teresa picked up the scissors.

The nape of the neck didn't need any noodling. And don't touch that cowlick, either.

Riding Clio, one hand on her mane.

"I'll be off now," Mrs. E. said, gathering the umbrella she used for the sun.

"You didn't finish your mousse," Teresa said. "Don't you know it's good for you? It's full of gelatin." Mrs. E.'s bones were peanut brittle; she walked with small steps. A visit to Hair Today was her personal best.

"Thank you, Mrs. Vardas, that's very kind. But I can see that you're busy and I'm in the way."

"Give me . . . serenity," Willy said after she left. His legs were swinging.

"Give her a break," Teresa said sharply. "Everybody's got their drug. Especially *you*," she added, shooting him a dark look.

Clio looked at Willy with sudden interest. Clio looked at a lot of things with interest, I liked that about her.

We'd gotten physical a few more times since the first night, once over at her place on the second floor of an airless ten-unit. It was the size of a bread box and smelled like it, too. My place was better. I didn't have to get up out of bed afterward, and then she'd gone right home. The last time, though, she'd sort of spent the night.

Things were going better in the performance department.

"Did you bring it?" I asked her reflection in the mirror.

"Of course."

Teresa laid down her scissors as though she had something important to say. "Clio, I want your opinion. I was thinking of getting an espresso machine. You know, one of those home models? I thought it might bring in a more sophisticated clientele. What d'ya think?"

Teresa used to ask me that type of question.

"Has everyone heard the latest? Some developer just bought twelve acres on top of Lucas Street," Willy announced. "It looks like they'll be razing the homeless camp there."

"Where Beanie lives?"

"You call that living?"

"You know what?" Teresa said. "Beanie was right about those gut germs he was always talking about. Gloria asked her biology professor and he confirmed they're being used in the food industry." Teresa laid her hand on Clio's shoulder. "Gloria's passion is food. She's going to turn pro soon and hates the idea she might make people sick. She's dying to meet you. She was going to come by today but she's busy making jam. Natal plum."

"Nepal?"

"Natal."

Teresa picked up the remains of the kiwi mousse and carried it outside. She came back a couple of minutes later, forehead troubled. "The birds don't want it," she said.

Clio laughed. "She should take out a patent: Gloria's Kiwi Mousse Pigeon Repellent. Apply to your window ledge."

Teresa gave Clio a long, searching look, then crossed the room at a trot and picked up the scissors again. She turned Clio's head this way and that. Perfection was always a shaft of hair away. Clio's head was becoming an obsession.

Don't touch that cowlick.

"How's it going, the two of you?" Teresa asked all of a sudden. Clio and I exchanged startled looks. Teresa's feelers rotated. "You know—the rock 'n' roll résumé," she added dryly.

"I guess we'll know soon enough," I said, getting up. I took my time rinsing out my coffee cup.

The cost of Clio.

I turned to her. "Come by when you're finished?"

I threw the mail on my desk, picked out a late-notice bill distractedly and studied the wording. You never knew what you could steal for your work—a turn of phrase here, an innuendo there.

Clio had style, all right. Some of her flower work—especially her charcoals—was surprisingly graphic. The dogs were another matter. I guess she didn't feel them. Maybe she wasn't meeting the right dogs.

I put the bills in a pile for Teresa and sorted through the rest. A donations drive for the Philharmonic. A newsletter from my college. How had they found me? They always found me. There was another letter from Mrs. Bing, in a pink scented envelope. I tossed it in the wastebasket unopened, along with the rest. Jeez. People were so literal. The broken home was just an idea. At least she'd laid off the cakes.

Willy had two letters, one from the Republic of Czech and another from the Philippines, plus the latest issue of *Beautiful Brides.*

I opened the letter from the Czech.

Darling Will [it read],

I do not know how many times I have teld myself to write this letter, and now I have did it. The vein in my heartache has growed too big and I am afraid it will break except I know. How many letters you have send my dear Will? I know, because I count. Twenty-two is how many. Yet still I wonder how it is that you not coming to a visit. We have got so close—sometimes I think too much close—but I do not feel the touch of you.

Is there a problem Will? Why is that you do not come? Tell me, my Will, you with so handsome words and sad eyes, will you not come? Otherwise I am so sorry. This would be so sad for me, but I will have to tie your letter with a ribbon and put you on a shelf and look down the path for a open man to hold, for I am young and that is what I have to give and give soon. Please Will deliver to me what is in your heart.

Your faraway girl,
Karelina

I threw the two letters in the in-box and picked up the issue of *Beautiful Brides*. The magazine was one of our regulars. Addresses were free with a one-year subscription. There were no limits on the girls.

I was just settling into the cover story on an eighteen-year-old Hungarian and her pepper seed collection when Clio knocked and poked her head around the connecting door.

I waved her over to the client seat. I stayed where I was. I wanted to keep this professional. She was thinking the same thing. We were a couple of briefcases.

"So tell me," she asked conversationally as she sat down, "what's Willy's drug?"

"That was indiscreet of Teresa," I fielded as I realized suddenly that *Beautiful Brides* was still on the desk! I swept it and a few other documents into my top drawer. She hadn't noticed. "I'm going to have to talk to her about that," I continued. "That's something you need to know if you do work for me: mum's the word when it comes to our clients."

Her voice rose a pitch. "He's a client? Really? What do you do for him?"

I zipped my lips.

"You're his drug dealer," she laughed.

I laughed back. When the laughter died, I said, "All right. Let's see it."

She pulled out the layout for Riff's résumé and spread it on the desk.

It was a cut-and-paste job. It was garish.

"Kinda flashy, isn't it?" I said, peering through splayed fingers.

"That's right," Clio said, plopping down next to it an issue of *Platter Patter,* the record industry trade magazine. "It's a parody. Everyone in the industry will get it. This is the original. I imagine you'll want to refer to it."

NEW TALENT HITS INDUSTRY, the headline of her layout read. Below was a photo of a handsomely suited torso, head lopped off, behind a huge teak desk. Riff's oversized, pierced head now rose over the executive's padded shoulders.

"Everyone will be guessing who's the decapitated exec," Clio enthused. "There'll be a buzz."

"Looks like *MAD* magazine."

"That's the way it's supposed to look. It's supposed to be fun. Fun," she repeated, vexed.

I had to admit, she'd captured Riff's personality. I was sure he'd love it. She'd used his hair as a design element. His spikes radiated all over the page. "All right," I said. A small smile escaped me. The thing practically jumped off the table.

Clio relaxed. "Here, let me show you how it's organized." She started to come over to my side of the desk, but I cut her off and came around to the client side. "These are the sub-heads," she said. "Of course, you'll come up with better lines, these are just indications." Our heads came together over the mock-up. Her breasts swung free under her T-shirt as she leaned over the desk.

I inched closer. "You didn't dress for work."

"I hope you're kidding," she replied and moved on. "A SERIES OF HITS is where you put Riff's past jobs and accomplishments. FOR THE RECORD is where you put his personal statement . . ."

"Hold it," I interrupted. "You didn't allow enough room for the text, not at that size type. What d'ya got there—twelve point?"

"No one reads the text. The important thing is the visual. That's the kick that gets in the door."

Teresa came in. She didn't knock. Clio and I edged apart.

"Hi you two. Don't let me interrupt." She sat down in her corner, pulled out a file and opened her ears.

My stomach wasn't sitting right. "It reads like an ad," I told Clio.

"Well, it *is* an ad in a way," Clio said. "An ad for a human being." Then she added, as if it were more palatable, "A professional product."

I looked over at Teresa. She was holding herself like a lightning rod. I couldn't stand it anymore. There was too much in the room. Where were the pigeons while we were at it? "Teresa," I said, "I'm sorry to have to ask, but I need some privacy here. Could you come back later this afternoon?"

"Of course, Joe," she said in a hurt voice. She left.

Jesus Christ.

I looked at my watch. Six more hours till the weekend. I needed emptying. I went back to my side of the desk. Clio looked at me with surprise.

I cleared my throat. "Now where were we?"

"My next assignment," she said.

I cleared my throat again. "Aren't you jumping the gun a little? How do I know Riff's going to like it? Just because I like it doesn't mean he will. Remember, I told you before: no guarantees. Anyway, at the moment I don't have anything for you," I said with a thin smile, holding up my hands. Then, just to be sure: "Don't give up your dog job."

Her eyes narrowed. It was true, I'd overdone it. "Don't worry," she said finally. She began, slowly, to gather her pencils and erasers. She used the same erasers I did, the kind you knead.

"Electra 90," she said, pointing to the *Platter Patter* headline. "The body is Tenneson." One eyebrow moved up. "Twelve point."

"I didn't mean to disparage your dogs," I said.

"No, of course not," she agreed. "That's not what you meant."

I closed a hand over hers as she reached for her pencil case. This was not how I planned it. "How's the big commission coming along?" I asked, low on the register. She'd gotten a job a week ago to draw six dogs of a wealthy client.

"I was supposed to start today on the Spinone," she said. Her voice was as measured as her T-square, but it warmed up as she went along. "I played with it yesterday to get acquainted but now they told me they had to take it to the clinic suddenly to get its sperm pumped. Something about elevated body temperature. I'm going to have to do the Bullmastiff instead. Cold."

"A Spinone? I've never heard of it."

"That's why it's getting its sperm pumped."

"Well, then."

She got up to go. "Are we still on?"

"Of course," I said, a little irritated. "Around eight okay? I've got something to take care of first."

She stood there. "I'm having car trouble again," she said.

"Need a lift to your client's?"

"I can walk. I'll have to—there's no bus to the top of the hill. But I can walk."

"I'll give you a lift."

"Maybe you could give me a ride back. That would be really great. I could get there okay."

"Sure. What time."

"Six okay? Really? That's so great." She gave me the address, it wasn't far away, and then she remembered: "Did you ask about the garden?"

"Yeah. It's no problem."

Clio's smile broke through the low clouds that had gathered in the office. She had a dazzler. I'd have to remember: all you had to do was promise her a garden.

Willy came in just as she was going out the door. She gave him a searching look. I sucked on my cheek.

I found her more interesting than her work.

Now it was Willy who gave me a look. "What does she want?" he asked as he sat down.

"The short answer is: none of your business," I said, a little sharply.

"She working for you?"

"She's just giving me a hand with a résumé. Don't worry. Nothing's changed."

He grunted.

I showed him the letter from the Czech. "The vein in my heartache?" he said after a minute, looking up at me.

"A local idiom," I shrugged. "So what'll it be? The usual?"

"Yeah."

I told him he'd gotten a new letter from Corazon, too, but he said he'd wait to read it till I'd written the reply. Willy liked to have his correspondence packaged.

He went off to finger *Beautiful Brides* while I started the Dear Jill to Karelina.

I always wondered for whose sake these letters were intended: the Jills', Willy's, or mine. Willy didn't have to answer; they were costing him money with no hope of return. But in general we acted like gentlemen and let the ladies save face. I'd written up a standard Dear Jill that seemed to fit every situation, so it was just a matter of copying it. Occasionally, if we'd particularly liked the girl, I'd add a personal touch.

Karelina was nothing special.

I pulled out a plain sheet of typewriter paper, crumpled it, then smoothed it back flat.

Nothing special. I smoothed the paper some more.

Clio had left her eraser on the desk. I knew it was hers, because it had lost its elasticity. Its surface was dark with graphite. I liked to keep mine clean.

I picked it up, pressed it so hard the muscles in my forearm bulged. These erasers were hard to soften once they'd clenched up, but little by little the rubber began to yield. First with the heel of my palm, then with my thumb, I flattened the eraser into the desk until the pale of the interior showed through the cracks. Then I folded it down the middle, doubled it back on itself, and began to knead, folding it always back onto itself—press, stretch, fold; press, stretch, fold— till the surface became satiny again and fresh and clean.

When the eraser was in order, I put it in my drawer and took out a pen.

Dear Karelina,

I would like to say that your last letter was a shock to me, but unfortunately that is not the case. I have been meaning to write you a frank letter in order to explain my situation, but I kept holding off—hoping against hope that my financial difficulties would be resolved and that I could visit you at last and make you my own, and that I would not find myself, as I do now, in the throes of bankruptcy court.

I won't go into details, which are tedious and cold and only

serve to remind me how I am severed forever from the warmth
and softness of you. Suffice it to say that the literary profession
as a whole has fallen into bad times, and I am afraid I was no
better than the others at stabilizing the shaky foundation. But
here's how it is: I have lost my home in the hills. I have lost my
office lease. Worst of all, I have lost my self-respect. I am now
living in my car.

I could never ask you to share a life that seems headed for
the streets.

I want to keep this short. I just want you to know that your
letters have shown me a glimpse of what love can be, a shaft of
light in the dark of my soul. I will carry your light with me the
rest of my days. You will be my measure of woman.

You must go on now and find yourself another man. It will
not be difficult, given your uncommon beauty and character. I
beg of you, Karelina, to think of me not with anger or frustration, nor even as a fallen man, but as someone you've touched
indelibly with your humanity and grace. I will remain your
unrequited lover forever.

> Remember me please,
> your Will

I folded the letter, slipped it into an envelope and took it
out to the sidewalk. I was smudging the envelope, to match
the crumpled letter, when Carlos Espinosa pulled up to the
curb in front of my door. In a car, a running car.

In better shape than mine.

"Hey, how you doin', sir!" He jumped out, leaving the car
in idle. He looked at my feet and the envelope beneath. He
didn't ask. I didn't offer.

"What's up?"

"I got a job!" he thrilled. He handed me a ten spot, and another sack of oranges. "Can you put that on the tab?" he asked, then he sprinted back to his car. "I owe you!" he waved from behind the steering wheel.

It was a hot afternoon, too hot for mid-May. I turned on the fan full blast. Unsecured letters fluttered in the in-box as though voices from overseas. Will, Will, they warbled. Whip-Poor-Will.

Teresa was over in her corner, reading a hairdo magazine. I could see its pages peeking out from under the account books. They were trembling in the breeze, too.

"How's the billing coming along?" I asked.

"Fine," she said, shifting positions.

The letter on the top of the in-box was fluttering the most. It was Corazon calling.

I brought out Corazon's file and reviewed our past notes and letters. This was her third letter already. I studied the new photograph she'd sent, then placed it on the table next to the earlier one. She was still dressed as a Catholic schoolgirl, complete with kneesocks — an unusual choice for someone in textile design. But either the skirt had been shortened since the prior letter or else Corazon had grown three inches in three weeks. Promising. There was a marked change, too, in her body language and pose. She was leaning against a wall on a tropical side street, next to an open door.

What was the name of that military base near Manila. Mabina?

I turned on the radio, there was a double-header today. I guess I could goof off, too. I was the boss.

The Asian was pitching. He was hot.

"This bother you, Teresa?"

"No, no."

In one corner of Corazon's letter was a dried, encrusted flower.

Dear Will

Thank you so much for your new photograph! You such a dark dreamboat. I know it's no good to say that. That put me wide open. But I look into your dark eyes and they look so sad I want to do things to make them smile. I hope you don't mind, but you maybe too thin, too. I want to feed you up. I make many delicious Filipino dishes. I make them and blow their flavors to you and you open your mouth and lick them up because you as wide as a stick of bamboo and I want to make your bamboo big.

I send you new picture of me, too, in front of the clothes company where I am put off. I don't know what I going to do, for I have very little dollars, but I am hard worker and I find another job soon. I know I can't want a Filipino man to help me. They are so weak. Maybe it is because they don't know who they are and if you don't know who you are, how do you know where you going? It is not their faults. We have been Spanish, we have been American, we have thirty different peoples and ninety languages and I think we are lost. But I stop talking about here. It is so dull and America is so fun! Anyway, my peoples are lost, but not me. I am just alone. When I get your letters I press them to my heart. Sometimes I am scared I so happy with your words and pictures that I feel warm inside.

I know what you mean, Will, when you say children act like babies sometime and get in way when us adults want to play. I am still young and have lots of play in me and am not ready to have children, maybe not never. For someone like you with your artistic temper, I understand it is hard to have babies in the house. You need your quiet. You have so many important things to think about like the nature of love and the complete-ness of Man and Woman, and you should not be bother with baby spit. I wish you tell me more about your litterature. What kinds of novels you write?

Sometimes late at night I think of those rubs you write me about. It is so long since I have rub. I remember my Daddy. He is rubbing my back when I am very, very little, when I wake up crying in the night.

I am a little scared being alone and no job and no money, but I am strong and will survive. I love Life no matter what it gives and I love your letters. *Please, please* keep writing. You don't be scared of being so much older than me. If okay with me, why not okay with you? I like old men. They remember me of when I am Daddy's little girl, before he is losing in the ferry sink, when everything in my world is right.

Do you think it okay if I ever call you Daddy?

Your Filipina girl,
Corazon

I got up, opened the door to the street. A rush of air came in, along with the scent of diesel and the report of a boom box. From the park came the honk of a donkey, guess it didn't like getting taken for a ride.

"You mind the noise, Teresa?" I asked over my shoulder. It would be hard to concentrate between the donkey and baseball and all, but it wouldn't affect my work. At the moment all I had to do was feel.

Teresa said it didn't matter since anyway she was finishing up. I asked her to pick up an international money order for thirty dollars when she got a chance and could she also remember our little discussion of yore about keeping a lid on the work at Joe's Word?

"What do you mean? I haven't said anything."

I didn't answer.

I stayed in the doorwell awhile longer after she left. There was some sort of crisis next door. The dentista raced past me to the Clinica Medica and then raced back again with another white frock in tow. It couldn't have been all that serious. There was no call for an ambulance.

I returned to my desk, my old garage-sale desk. It was ringed with wet glass marks and carved with the initials JB. I'd never known whether its owner was Joe Blow or an alcoholic. Maybe he was both.

My dear Corazon,

I can't begin to describe the intense pleasure you gave me when you asked if you could call me Daddy. To think that someone as sweet as you might think of me in this way and look up to me for protection and education in the ways of the world — I, who have been so isolated from the love and warmth a family affords! This is a new stage in our still-evolving connection, one which holds the promise of great fullfillment. Yet I must also admit that it is one I embark upon with some trepidation. For as much as I would love to hold you in my arms and call you my baby girl and help you navigate

through life, I know what others may say of such a union.
There are those who would not approve of a bond not sanc-
tioned by the official processors of morality.

Morales stole third base. Three and 2, two out . . . Bunt to
the right infield! Morales was running . . . Morales was running . . . Morales was out.

It is you I am thinking about. Have you the spirit to defy
convention? My dear Corazon, when I see that last snapshot of
yours, I want to set those pleats in your skirt right, to smooth
the troubles life has unjustly thrown your way. Please accept
the enclosed money order as a small sign of my concern, and
with the money in your pocket go buy some wholesome food
and make those native dishes you wrote me about and eat
them yourself so that you stay plump and healthy and full of
cheek. My little girl.

You ask about my writing. I will tell you a little but you
must not ask too much, for to talk about one's writing is
almost a betrayal of oneself. I want my work to express who I
am, not the other way around. But since you ask:

My characters are your next-door neighbors, husbands,
wives, outcast politicians and car thieves, all caught in the
web of desire, of love and the death of love, of greed and the
limbo state. Whether they live in L.A. or on the frozen Russian
steppes, their condition is universal and timeless and for that,
my work never ends. I am always digging for the truth. I know
it's there somewhere, beyond the drill of nine-to-five and the
numbing of material consumption, but the closer I get, the
more I hurt. The glare of truth is always hard to look at; most
people avert their eyes. Maybe that's why I've always steered

clear of personal contact. I've never found anyone sensitive
and brave enough to share the emotional burden of an artist's
life. I have often wondered if I myself have the guts to go on.
But that is the life of an artist, one prolonged stifled sob.

It is a wonder to me that I am nonetheless fairly successful,
that others are willing to pay me good money to write so that I
may live out my *angst* in a modestly comfortable house, along
with a garden to inspire me and keep me in contact with the
fundamentals of life.

Pollen, seed, swollen fruit: what is ambition next to this?

I hope you don't mind my baring my soul. You seem so
sensitive and receptive, so unlike the California women I meet
who give me allergies.

Corazon, you have painted a sorry picture of yourself alone
in bed with no one to massage you through your bad moments
and help you slip back to sleep. Remember when you told me
about your favorite body part? You liked your belly button
because it made you feel connnected, even though your connections have long since passed away? Will you do me a favor?
Will you imagine me there beside you on the edge of your bed?
Imagine me there and rub your belly—and the area around
your belly—and then I believe something electric will happen,
something cosmic. Because I believe we are meant to connect,
the way an electron fuses to a proton, the way a fat bee is drawn
to a flower that sways in a heavy breeze. I hope you believe this,
too, that we are a force meant to join together, to forge a new
beginning based on complicity and trust.

Corazon, my little Filipina, I believe if you imagine me there
beside you, you will fall into a deep and dreamless sleep, emptied of all your fears and tensions, knowing you are loved by
                          Your Daddy

I read it over to be sure I'd rung all the bells, then I marked the time on Willy's chit.

Shoot. It was 6:15 already.

Fourteen

The lowering sun hit square against my windshield as I headed west on Sunset, and the air blowing in through the open windows offered little relief. Beads of sweat trickled down my back about the same speed as the traffic. I was late, I was wilted, and—I lifted a shoulder—no, I didn't smell.

What the hell. I turned right at the next intersection and tried my luck on surface streets.

But that was even worse. The outcrop of small, steep hills in neighboring Silverlake made for a maze of narrow, twisting streets alive with residents unloading provisions for the weekend, socializing with neighbors, walking the dog. It was slow going. The higher I went, the steeper the lots and the bigger the homes. Some of them were real cliff-hangers. I guess that's why everyone drove four-wheel drives.

That was the middle class. As I continued to climb, the landscaping thickened and houses fell away. The dog lady's house was so high on the hog, you couldn't even see it. It was behind a wall. I supposed she drove a helicopter.

"I'm here to pick up Clio," I told an electronic panel at

the entry gate. I got a crackle for a response, then slowly the gates cranked open. The driveway was one of those meandering affairs meant to stun the visitor with a major manor beyond a bend. Only here there was no mansion; nothing was visible at all at the end except a long colonnade of marble framed by a pair of cedars. I could leave my mark here, I thought as I switched off the engine, and it would probably be a grease spot. The place was hopelessly clean, a real Mt. Olympus. In fact, I half expected a deity to appear—and I wasn't disappointed. A tawny blonde in a wispy gown swept towards me out of nowhere, Clio in her wake. A gust of wind lifted her trailing veils, as if she'd staged her approach.

I stayed put. What was my choice? The three hundred pounds of Bullmastiff and Afghan that'd been hounding me since I crossed the gates were slamming their fat paws against my door, snarling, showing me their canines.

"Shamus! Rockwell! Down boys, down!" the dog lady called from a distance. She didn't rush to my rescue.

As she leaned over to calm the dogs, a coil of hair tumbled over her face and played with the last rays of the sun.

"Nice welcome," I said to her finally, when it was safe to get out. "Hi, Clio."

The dog lady brushed the sunlight aside. "Don't you like dogs?" she said airily. She held out a hand. "My name's June, June Barry."

"I'm Joe."

"Of course. I've heard so much about you from your charming girlfriend," she said. I looked at Clio. Clio looked at the gravel. "But she didn't tell me you were so . . ." she chose her words with care, ". . . so dark."

"You mean hairy?" I asked.

Her shoulders lifted an inch. "I bet you could use a drink," she answered, pointing to the half-moons under my armpits.

"Thanks, but we have to get going."

"I'd like to make you a proposition," she countered. "How about hearing me out while we toast the weekend? What can I offer you? Wait—let me guess. You're scotch on the rocks."

"You're dating me."

"Am I?" Mrs. Barry laughed. Clio looked back and forth between our faces. "Well, we have a full bar," she went on, "including some wicked sinsemilla. How about it, Clio?"

"I'm sorry. It can't be done," I said, looking at Clio. She'd been so quiet. "I've got someone to see."

"Let me put it to you now, then, and you can be on your way. We can always talk through the details later. I want to give my husband a memoir for his birthday."

Far off in the basin a siren was pushing its way through the city. Up here it was so quiet you could hear the irrigation drip.

"Clio told me what kind of a writer you are," she continued, "and of course I wanted to meet you. You see, I've heard this sort of thing exists—ghost-written memoirs—but I didn't know anyone who'd do them. Apparently they're easy enough. You do one long interview to set up the theme and then it's just a matter of four or five follow-ups. Plus of course the writing part."

"Who's your husband?"

She took a long sip of her drink. "Art Barry," she said.

"The TV anchor? Can't you get a regular publisher interested?"

"To be perfectly honest, my husband's had a pretty dull life," she said. "But he's had his achievements and I'm sure you could make them interesting. That's where the art is, no? Shamus! Down boy!"

"I didn't like these pants anyway. Look, Mrs. Barry . . ."

"Call me June—and don't worry: you won't be writing about the dogs. The dogs are *my* story."

"But you don't know me from Adam, you don't know how I write, and . . ." She started to object again but I wouldn't hear it. ". . . I don't have the time."

"I wish you'd think it over. Clio can assure you I'll make it worth your while." She pressed my hand again. "It's so nice to meet you. See you Tuesday, sweetie," she added to Clio. She urged us both a great weekend.

Halfway down the hill, Clio said, "I thought you wouldn't mind."

"I don't mind," I said.

I took her along. I had to. It was dusk already.

Aldo Missoni met us at the curb in front of his sagging bungalow. "Is this Mrs. Joe?" he stage-whispered over the hood. Aldo had a tire around his waist that he carried with grace and a pair of suspenders, but tact wasn't his strong suit.

Clio went directly to the mutilated topiaries. "The poor things," she said. "What were they? Will they come back?"

"Rabbits, the louts!" Aldo bristled. He stroked the stub of an ear.

"What kind of trees are they?"

I interrupted. "Excuse me, Clio, but I've got to get a move on." I pointed to a rose bush with a fender wrapped around it. "Is this the latest rubbish?" I asked Aldo. He nodded and showed me the other damage, and then he and Clio resumed their topiary talk while I took photographs. The light was dim, I had to use a low F-stop.

There was little activity on the street at the moment. A couple of grease monkeys played with their tools at the freeway sound wall, but their work hadn't spilled over this far. According to Aldo, the real crunch came on Monday mornings when whole caravans of cars dragged in. Then the block looked like a bad hangover.

Aldo went into the house to get the letters. He brought back a plate of cookies, too. *"Biscotti?"* he offered. He didn't have much money, but he had hospitality.

I sat down on the porch steps in the failing light to read the latest LAPD travesty. I had to squint.

Dear Mr. Missoni:

Regarding your letter of April 17th, I can fully understand your frustration at the circumstances you describe. Yet I hope you realize that you offer no proof of your allegations. *A priori* you cannot pester people who may just be doing a good deed for their father-in-law, or tightening a screw for a friend down the street.

However, we at the LAPD Rampart Division take all citizen's complaints seriously, and so I have talked to your local patrol who know the area and know the tensions that arise between ethnic groups. They have suggested that meeting with these men face-to-face and simply talking through your differences might diffuse the situation without having to resort to name calling and possible libel charges. Concretely, they suggest that you share a meal of tacos together.

I think it's an excellent suggestion. Much can be accomplished through simple citizen goodwill. I wish you the best of luck.

>Sincerely,
>Sergeant Ramsey

I laughed, a rich, dark *mole* laugh. I loved the libel touch.

I looked up. Clio seemed happy as a bug. Aldo was showing her his stunted shrub collection. I hadn't noticed it before—guess I wasn't thinking along those lines—but everything in the yard had been tortured. Guide wires were everywhere, limbs were lashed to the ground with prongs. In the deep twilight you could just make out a faint metallic glimmer crisscrossing the lot. It looked like the web of some terrible creature.

I shook my head. My mind was going Gothic. Damn gripe letters.

I opened the second letter.

The response from the 13th Council District was frosting on the *mole*.

Dear Constituent:

Thank you for your recent letter concerning your problem. We have created a file and will look into it. It is in your interest in the meanwhile to report any activity directly to the police.

>Sincerely,
>Councilwoman Barbara Hasfeld

Aldo and Clio had disappeared. I was just getting up to look for them when they came around the side of the house. Clio was carrying something, something hairy and Gothic. She waved them at me. "Cuttings!" she trilled.

I waved the letters at Aldo. "Look, Aldo," I told him. "You've read the letters. Why go on?"

"I can't stop now—not after everything I've done! I'll never give up! Never! I'll kill those assholes! Pardon my French," he bowed to Clio.

It was none of my business; I could walk away. But in fact, I was afraid it would end in murder if I threw it back at Aldo. "You collect your own documents from now on then," I said at last. "Start a log. Note the time of any event, any details, any conversation you overhear. Find out how the customers heard about these guys. Try to get a picture of money changing hands—and the license plate numbers in those three A.M. hauls. But for Christ's sake, Aldo, be discreet. These men are going to protect their livelihood." I sighed at the futility of it all. "What you really need is to slip some money to the police. It'd be cheaper in the long run than paying me, and a whole lot more effective."

"I'll be damned if I do that. That's why I left Italy. This is America!" Aldo snapped his suspenders. Then he said, "Maybe Beanie can help take notes."

Clio and I turned our heads.

"I was just kidding, I'd never ask. But some nights he's been sleeping in the bushes there by the freeway sound wall."

How hard could Beanie be on himself? This was a new low.

"Have they shut down the Lucas Street camp already?"

"Not that I know of."

"No, not yet."

The three of us were sitting on the steps of Aldo's bungalow, shooting the breeze about Beanie, when a patrol car glided silently by in the near dark, and came to a stop at the end of the road. A moment later the engine was killed.

"Wait here," I said, getting up.

I kept low, moving from bush to bush, closing in on the shrubbery at the foot of the dead end. I didn't have to worry about making noise; even when I reached the thicket and stumbled over a piece of cardboard—Beanie's bed?—nothing was audible above the traffic's drumming thunder.

The street lamps were starting to turn on but there must've been a glitch, because the light was fitful and had no force. Its liverish glow cast ghastly shadows inside the leaf canopy. I crouched close to the earth, parted the foliage and peered out onto the street.

One of the homeboys was leaning over the window of the patrol car, deep in conversation with the driver. I couldn't catch their drift but I could hear their laughter.

The cops didn't stay long. I froze as the headlights swung past my hiding place, illuminating for an instant the crate at my feet.

Clio and Aldo wanted to know if I'd seen anything.

"No, nothing," I said, shaking my head. "Nothing unusual."

Fifteen

Clio left the cuttings in the car while we walked down Sunset in search of a place to eat. Aldo had wrapped the twigs in a baggie. They'd be okay, she said.

The streetlights still fizzled and popped over our heads. It seemed all Echo Park was missing its connections, but somehow it seemed to energize the place. We were high-stepping it past the vacant lot next to the car wash when big-time pops exploded on the street. Pop. Pop. Pop. We hit the ground fast, but when we looked up we saw it was only the backfire from an Alternative Tours bus.

We got to our feet, hearts still thumping. The tourists stared at us out the windows, noses pressed against the glass. Clio gave them the finger as the bus moved off to other ghettos.

I wasn't happy, either, but why let the incident spoil the evening? I was hungry. "How about Les Frères, cherie?" I said as we passed its lot of Cadillacs and Lincolns and its facade of faux Basquerie.

"Your treat?" Clio was joking, too, at least I hoped she

was. Ed Hutch was outside, glad-handing his customers at the valet stand. We kept walking.

We nixed Pescadito's and Barragan's, too, before settling at last on Pescado Mojado. You had to eat out of Styrofoam but the tacos were cheap and the fish soup had bite.

I dived in. "Tilapia," I identified, though they called it something else.

"The fish that destroyed your marriage?"

"It's taken on whole ecosystems. We were just small fry. It escaped in Lake Nicaragua in the eighties."

"So much for Lake Nicaragua?"

"It's everywhere now."

"How can you eat it?"

"I'm an omnivore."

The place was popular with every sort, drunks from Los Piños here for menudo, neighborhood gringos, families of Asians and Latins, plus assorted machos biding time while their women prayed at the storefront church next door. If you wanted to, you could believe that it actually worked, a Third World community sharing tacos together.

Afterward Clio wanted to continue south of the border. She wanted to go to Los Piños. Not me.

"Why not? It'll be fun."

"It'll be murder."

As we neared the bar its pink doors swung open and a drunk spilled out, just like in the movies, except here you had the perfume of pee. The doors swung shut again. You couldn't see anything except a row of pant legs.

"I'll go on my own sometime, then," Clio said. "I'm not afraid."

"You don't belong there. Let them have a place of their own."

"Is this an Issue?"

"Yeah. An issue of good beer. I'm going to the Short Stop. You coming?"

You could hear Clio's mind turn a couple of clicks, but she decided to let it ride. It would kick up again, though, I was sure of it. We walked for a block without talking till we got to a spot where our progress was blocked. It was Beanie on his soapbox. Under the zapping streetlights he looked like a hallucination.

We fell into formation with the others upwind. When the wind shifted, so did the audience and then Beanie had to swivel, too. But that was part of his appeal. Beanie's happenings were spontaneous, organic; the crowd was part of the yeast.

He was up in the sky again.

". . . They own our land, they own our water, and now they've grabbed our air. But remember, today is your day! If someone's trying to steal your birthday cake, take it back!" He looked right and left, then tossed a handful of confetti high into the sky. It was quite an effect with the strobe lights.

"He's so sad," Clio whispered.

"Ever heard of the Smog Exchange? They made our air a commodity on the market and issued permits to pollute. Did they consult you?" Beanie pointed to his gyrating dollar.

"Noooo. They went the way the wind blows. There ought to be a law!" Beanie jabbed his umbrella into the air. "And there is: the law of the AQMD and LAPD and the CEO of Disneyland. It's the law of the land—of the rich and those who protect the rich—and now it's in the air!"

Though there were a few puzzled looks in the crowd at the mention of Disneyland, only a handful walked away when Beanie segued into the serious. Smog Exchange? The words circulated. Adults asked their kids to translate.

Beanie's alarm clock went off. He waved it above our heads. "Time to register!" he cried. "Remember the Party Platform: Arrest war. Kiss, don't kill. Talk back to your leaders. Watch your parking meters."

"Happy Birthday!" someone shouted.

I'd seen it before. They'd forget Beanie and his party five minutes after they left. His crowds were way down from the helicopter crash peak. I didn't know how he could keep it up.

". . . taken over the firmament, too. And you thought all there was in heaven was God's love? No siree Bob! The heavenly hosts are dodging satellites up there—thousands of satellites all owned by the M&M's, plus thousands of other pieces of debris left by other space missions. Some of that stuff up there is fueled by plutonium. And some of it is falling down. Remember Chicken Little? 'The sky is falling! The sky is falling!' He got an acorn on his noggin and we took him for a nut? Has it come to this, that we have to revise our fairy tales?"

Beanie's eyes filled. Was "Chicken Little" the Bible in baby

Beanie's nursery? Peel back the layers of Beanie and there were always more beneath.

"And the costs!" he exclaimed. "What about the health costs of nuclear fallout? Or the cost of a re-entry crash, a direct hit on a population? What about the literal costs of the programs, like the new 8X satellites at $1.5 billion each?

"That's money that could go instead to the Birthday Party so that every single person in this land could have a piece of birthday cake—and afford to go to the doctor afterward if they got a bellyache.

"Then there's the cost no one's talking about: the cost to our privacy. Those satellites aren't up there just to sell wireless pagers and TV. They're there to spy and eavesdrop. And blimps are next in line. At least they're not noisy, which is more than you can say for police helicopters which spy on us, too—with some of the same hardware. Like the microwave system that transmits video images to the ground. Who knows? They could take pictures one day of you and your neighbor fooling around."

The cops were here again. Clio and I exchanged looks. Beanie didn't seem to notice.

"The fact is, law enforcement chopper patrols are one of the main civilian consumers of the military's surveillance technology! And who persuaded our city to buy choppers in the first place? NASA, that's who. NASA."

"He's got a right to speak, doesn't he?" Clio whispered.

"He could be obstructing traffic."

"As for that wireless stuff, who says those emissions are safe? Satellites are beaming microwaves on our heads constantly. We're also getting it from right and left. You've seen the twirling rods, haven't you? the ones that've sprouted above billboards everywhere in order to relay cell calls?

"Preliminary research isn't encouraging and long-term effects aren't known. Yet most experts say wireless communication is perfectly safe. Can I have a show of hands here? How many of you believe the experts are funded by the Big Buckeroos? Raise your hand if you belong to the Birthday Party!"

Beanie's face glowed at the response.

The cops tried to count hands, too, but the crowd was keeping them low, out of sight.

". . . transmission towers in Catholic schoolyards in poor and minority neighborhoods. And Congress last year, in a payback to lobbyists, made it illegal for local governments to reject projects on health grounds!"

They got out of their car. This time they held a pair of handcuffs. The crowd began to break up.

"Happy birthday to you, happy birthday to you . . ."

When the cops walked up and clamped the cuffs on him, Beanie seemed startled.

There were a half-dozen of us left. Clio seemed particularly upset. "What are you arresting him for?" she blurted out.

"The Katz law," the cop said. "No loitering in high-crime areas." He was stern, but not unpleasant. Just doing his duty.

"That hasn't gone into effect yet!" an old man exclaimed. It was the retiree with the fishing rod, only tonight he wasn't fishing. "Take those handcuffs off! Where'd you get your orders, young man?" He got out a pen and a small notebook from a pocket. "May I have your names and numbers, please?"

Beanie looked flabbergasted. He'd actually recruited a Party member.

The two officers frowned, conferred, then returned to the patrol car where they got on the buzzer. Three minutes later, they were back. They shoved the old man aside and pushed Beanie to the squad car, lowered his head, and threw him into the backseat.

The retiree sputtered with anger. "What are the charges!"

"It's illegal to sing 'Happy Birthday,'" the young officer said as he got behind the wheel. He could barely keep a straight face. "You can hum the tune but you can't sing the words. This could be a violation of intellectual property rights."

The patrol car squealed away. The old man was the first to speak. "'Happy Birthday'? You call that intellectual?"

Clio turned to me. "What are we going to do? What'll happen to Beanie? He could be hurt."

"Don't worry about him—he'll probably like it." I shrugged. "Nothing we can do about it. Let's go shoot pool."

I started off. Clio followed, trailing at first, storm clouds massed over her head under the crackling streetlights. First Los Piños, now Beanie.

It took a couple of beers and a fluke bank shot before she was able to forget.

Sixteen

Clio spent the morning at the nursery and when she returned she was loaded for bear: trowel, weeder, hand hoe, sacks of fertilizer and amendments, plus trays of seedlings and potted plants. She must've blown all her Riff's résumé money on the lot. At least I'd been able to borrow a pitchfork from the Chinese guy across the street.

I didn't know exactly how the garden had happened, but it had and Clio and I had come to terms. It was her dime and her time, she'd pointed out. I'd get to enjoy the garden. Everyone would—Suzette, George, Number 4. "No matter what" was never stated, though it was a major amendment and it was understood.

She was a little concerned about Sergeant. I'd told her I thought it'd be okay. I'd never seen him out unsupervised. Even George knew you couldn't play loose with a pitbull.

She started digging in the early afternoon. I watched for a while. She had to jump on the heel of the pitchfork to get below the Bermuda grass thatch, then heave out a wedge, throw it upside down and whack it with the back of the pitchfork again to loosen the soil from the sod. She attacked with the energy of a thirty-five-year-old but progress was by inches. She made me tired.

I went inside and made a dent in my periodicals, and when that made me sleepy I watched the ballgame. It was a good one. The season was still young and the players in control. I didn't care much for games at the end of summer. Too much was riding. Wagner, Tchaikovsky maybe. Not Bach.

During the seventh-inning stretch I stepped outside. Clio had finished beating the sod and was leaning on the pitchfork, panting. Clumps and wiry lengths of the grass were everywhere, including in her hair.

"I'll clean up after I get the plants in. Don't worry," she said.

I wiped a smudge of dirt off her shoulder. Her shirt was soaked. I handed her a glass of fresh-squeezed orange juice.

"The man at the nursery told me not to plant anything now. 'Too late,' he told me. 'Fall better.'"

"What'd you get?" I asked, looking down at her feet.

"Petunias, flax, lobelia, and verbena." She pointed them out. "They're all blue. You can't tell, but they will be. I'm planting yellow flowers for contrast." She showed me a design she'd devised. Aldo's lavender sticks would go under the bedroom window once they'd rooted. They'd be her bones, she said.

When I asked where the black and white plants were, she took me seriously and I heard more than I wanted about the failures of plant breeders to achieve true black and—even more problematic—why they wanted to in the first place. I retreated to my game.

An hour later she walked in the living room. She looked beat.

"That poor cat. It doesn't take its eyes off me. It hasn't moved all day. Why should I feel guilty?"

"You don't have to feel guilty. It's not your cat. Why don't you relax. Take a bath."

"Here?"

I got up and returned a minute later with my bathrobe. I tossed it to her. "I put out a towel for you, too, but the house doesn't provide bubbles."

She started singing the moment the water hit the tub, in that strong, cool voice of hers that wove over and under the *continuo* of the tap. Fluids were in the air. The apartment smelled wet. Then the damn phone rang and Sergeant next door started to yap. He'd never heard such a racket at my place.

I had to answer; Clio wouldn't understand.

It was Pete.

"You're home!" he said on the upbeat like he always did. "Not out making history?"

"It's Saturday, haven't you heard? History's on hold."

"Sorry to call on the weekend. I thought I'd catch you at the Brite Spot, but we haven't crossed lately."

"No we haven't. What's up, Pete?"

"Just calling to maintain morale—to review the latest scores and penalties in the game of life."

"What'd you need me for? You've got a wife."

"You know they're not players, it's not the same—Hey! What's that I hear in the background? Someone's singing *chez toi.* Some . . . one's . . . sing . . . ing," he sung, then he clicked his tongue, throwing in plenty of juice. "You old son of a gun. And here I'd thought you were an old fart. Shows me."

"She's a record. Maggy Wish—never heard of her? *Making Waves.* First album."

"Bring her by the Brite Spot."

"Hey, Pete, whatever happened with the helicopter crash? I haven't heard a thing about the investigation—not even a paragraph on page 12 in the *Times'* business section. Wasn't the National Transportation Safety Board supposed to give a report? It's been so long."

"The NTSB doesn't investigate when the weight of the aircraft is less than 12,000 pounds. The LAPD handles it. They can invite the NTSB and the FAA to help if they want. They didn't."

"The LAPD investigated itself?"

"Yeah. But the report wasn't publicized."

"How come? Couldn't they find the cause?"

"They found it all right. I read about it in the last issue of *Rotor and Wing.* The chopper wasn't hit by bullets; there was no mechanical failure, either. It was the pilot that malfunctioned. Human error."

I waited. "Well?" I asked when nothing was coming.

Pete grunted. "There was insufficient lift because of that canyon. The chopper was trying to ascend; it couldn't get enough power—too low in a confined area."

"You're kidding." My voice tightened. "Too low?"

"Human error."

"That's not an error in my neighborhood. That's policy."

You could hear his shrug.

"Thanks for the information, Pete. It's good of you to call," I said, "but I've got to go."

"Yeah, sure, I can understand. Have to go turn over that record."

"Get outta here."

"Hey, Joe, can you do me a favor? Can you get me Jenny's phone number? You don't mind, do you?"

I sat by the phone afterward, fingering the cushions.

The media could air the report, but it'd never do it. It was like Beanie said. The media, the rich and powerful, the cops: they all had a stake in helicopters. They'd buried the "accident" the day they'd buried the cops.

I got up and walked softly over to the bathroom door. The concert was over now but Clio was still humming. I peeked around the edge of the door. She was lying almost flat, soaking, the aureoles of her breasts lapped like islands by the waterline. I went back to the living room and waited on the love seat. The slap of water, the clink of the soap dish against ceramic: the sounds of intimacy carried into the living room in successive waves.

When she came out I handed her a beer and patted the cushion next to me. She sank down, chugged a stream of beer down her open throat. My bathrobe was too large for her and fell off one shoulder. "Ahh," she said. You could feel the velvet in her voice and that's how I was feeling, too, conditioned by the sounds of soap slipping and towel rubbing and my imagination.

"Who was that on the phone?" she asked.

"My mother," I told her.

She nodded, took another swig. She didn't ask anything more. I liked that about her. After that first night when she'd needed to believe, she'd never probed into my past.

I took Clio's hand, the one without the beer.

"You didn't get out all the dirt," I said after examination.

"You never do," she laughed. "They say eventually it gets into your blood."

"Is this your first garden? You didn't have one with the German?"

"Yes," she said. "I mean, no. We lived in an apartment." She drew her legs up onto the love seat suddenly and tucked them out of sight. "I've just had potted plants." One little toe stuck out. A very small baby toe.

"What happened there?" I pointed.

She seemed startled by that one, too, but then she extracted her feet and put them on my lap for inspection. "Both toes are that way," she said. "I used to be embarrassed about it, but then I read that the human race was evolving and it was the disappearance of the baby toe that was its most obvious manifestation. It has to do with humans not needing ape feet, something like that. So the way I see it now is that I appear to be one of the more evolved specimens of Homo sapiens on earth."

Defective baby toes. I stroked her flawed beauty. By now I had a fully evolved boner.

"I hardly ever get to explain all that," she smiled. "It takes so long. Most people just think that I have a defect."

I leaned over and started to nuzzle. "Relaxed?"

"Mmmm."

A moment later she said, "You know what I could really go for right now? A nice fat joint. A nice fat joint," she repeated wistfully.

She wasn't ready for mine, but I remembered the little package from Riff. I'd thrown it in the back of my dresser and forgotten all about it.

On the way back I stopped at the stereo and put on some mood music.

Clio's face lit up at the sight of the weed. "Where'd you get that? I thought you didn't smoke." She struck a match. "It's rolled like a pro."

"I lead a shadow life," I said, sitting back down and slipping a hand into the open fold of her/my bathrobe. I had the fleeting sensation I was playing with myself.

"I believe it. Anybody that embezzles."

"Embezzled."

I roamed the soft swell of her belly as she inhaled, and her belly button.

"How did your family react to your crime?" she asked. "What'd your mother say?"

I got up and changed the record. Hank Williams wasn't doing it. "She doesn't know," I said. "We disconnected long ago."

Her smile was small and a little detached, which was not in the direction I wanted to go, but I got busy and pretty soon I got a sigh out of her that I took for a green light although it could've been a sigh of fatigue or even resignation at my foul character. To tell the truth, I took it the way I wanted because I wasn't about to be stopped. I got up, kicked the front door shut, dropped to my knees, and started applying kisses to her other lips. And that did it, she lost her distance. Her mouth opened and she vacuumed me in. She rode me with her tongue up and down, over and around. And that was just my thumb. In the meanwhile I was getting a head massage that beat Teresa's any day. When I couldn't breathe anymore, I got back on my feet and pulled her to the next room and onto the bed.

She lay splayed before me: "The Origin of the World," her black snatch lit by the pale of her thighs like a piece of fine art.

"You're so hairy," Clio said, reaching out.

"I'm a throwback," I said as I straddled her, pinning her arms above her head. "Want another joint, Clio? A nice fat joint?"

"Yes, please. Puh-lumphhh."

"Junkie. Don't talk with your mouth full."

We laid like slag on the bed afterward, our heat and body musks slowly exchanging with the evening air that washed through the open window. Clio told me the name of the tree we were smelling, the one in the vacant lot with the scent of orange blossoms. For me, it was a new kind of pillow talk.

When we finally moved it was from hunger. I found some meat loaf in the ice box I'd made earlier and we started to nibble on that, and then this and that, and before long it became clear we had just eaten dinner and there was no question we were spending yet another night together, two nights in a row. With relief we dropped the hesitations and half-measures that smelled of bad tango and plopped down in front of a tape of *Breathless*. We compared Seberg's haircut to Clio's, of course, and did rubbery things with our lips that gave me another spasm down south, but it was brief and when we went to bed well past midnight it was to sleep.

We got up late the next morning. It was a beautiful day, much cooler than the day before. The first thing Clio did was bend over and visit her plants. "Do you think they've grown?" she asked. She groaned theatrically as she straightened out and complained of being stiff. I told her to sit tight and relax while I made breakfast, but ten minutes later, when I lowered the flame on the bacon and brought out a cup of fresh brew, she was outside on the stoop starting a sketch.

She didn't know the first thing about doing nothing. There was an art to it, but like all disciplines you needed to practise.

"I always carry a sketchbook in my purse," she explained. "It's just a quick sketch; I want to have a 'before' record of the garden." She was working in pencil, a cheap mechanical pencil. Her sketch pad was small and light, its paper cheap. "This is not for posterity," she said when she saw I'd noticed. " 'After' is for posterity."

"Want a picture of yourself in front of the 'before' bed?" I asked.

She beamed at me till I remembered I'd finished off the roll of film at Aldo's. Her eyes were gray with breaks of cream and brown in them like nougat. They were disturbing in the strong light.

"That's all right," she said, crushed. "I'll have the sketch. A sketch is always better and I'll be in the picture anyway, in a way, because I am the picture."

". . . and I'm your waiter and my name is Joe. This is your coffee," I pointed out. "You need it."

I served the bacon and eggs on the steps and she put down the sketch while we ate, but when I brought out a second cup of coffee a half hour later, she'd picked it up again and now Sergeant lay scratching his fleas at her feet.

The sketch was starting to hold together. She'd put Number 4's apartment across the way in the picture, too, and why not? There wasn't a whole lot to draw in the "before" bed. In the background, with a light touch that conveyed distance, were Number 4's big-screen TV and catatonic cat.

"I'm cheating, you know," she told me as she thanked me for the refill. "The really great botanical illustrators spent hours observing before they lifted their pen. Of course, I'm not drawing a plant, I'm drawing a scene, but you should do it for scenes, too."

"They still exist?"

"Botanical illustrators? Yes, they're still around. Scientific journals need them. A photograph can't show both the volume of a plant and its details at the same time. Either everything is in focus and flat, or else only one point is in focus and the rest is fuzz. Plus it's no good to just replicate a plant. If you showed everything, you'd end up with a million black dots that'd smudge together in the printing process. That's why you need the insight and perception of a human being. You have to decide what can be suggested. Some botanial illustrators are real artists. Nicolas Robert, Francis Bauer: it's amazing what can be done with pen and ink!"

"Color is so cheap," I said.

Clio smiled. "It can blind you to form. I don't have the patience, or maybe the talent, to do that kind of work," she continued. "Anyway, if there were ever a demand for a drawing, which is rare, an editor would call one of the botanical illustrators. My drawings aren't really exact. They're more a point of view. I add certain things. And mostly, I leave things out."

"Here comes the void."

"It's true. It's not what you do, it's what you don't."

"I believe you," I said. She was getting serious on me again. I stared at the ground and pretended to be absorbed.

"Most people think of art as an expression," she said, gathering steam, "but I feel that to really express what you want to say you have to *repress*. Of course you can go too far. A lot of art is so abstracted, it's precious. That's why I love plants—you can't get more grounded. The personal and the particular, framed by space and . . ."

There, in the shade of a rusty hibachi grill, two lizards were copulating. They were motionless; it was by chance my eyes happened to fall on them. The male held the female beneath him with his claws; his jaws were clamped on her neck. An occasional blink of her eyes, an occasional twitch of his hind legs: these were the only movements, and they didn't seem related.

". . . yet the vacuum has volume and shape, since it's the spaces between the volumes that define form. If it didn't exist, a form would have nowhere to move, or anywhere to be. That's why it's so touching, a void. It's intangible."

She waited for my reaction.

I lifted my head, pointed to her drawing. "That's all in there?"

"Sure, it's there. But it's been swallowed by the void." Then she laughed.

I reached out and gave her neck a little caress. "Look," I said and pointed to the lizards, and for a while we were quiet and watched nothing happen.

I wondered if Clio liked me because she saw the void in me.

"Clio," I said finally, as lightly as I could make it. "I've got some plans for today . . ."

"Me, too," she said. She closed her sketchbook. "You're right, it's time to get going. I can finish this during the week when you're at work, when I won't be in the way." She got up, went inside.

I followed her. "You're not in the way," I said like an idiot.

She gathered her purse and her portfolio of dog work from Friday, then turned in a little circle, surveying the room. "Am I forgetting anything?" she asked, and then she remembered her garden supplies.

She managed to clear a space in her purse for the fish fertilizer and the trowel, but there was still the hand hoe and the weeder and the half-empty sack of manure to go. She started to juggle, but I told her to stop. I went outdoors and searched for a place where her supplies would be safe. I looked high and low, but none existed.

"There's some space under the kitchen sink," I said at last. "I suppose you can leave them there."

Clio frowned. "But how would I get to them? I could only garden when you're here?"

There was a long silence. We both looked at the ground. This time there were no lizards to watch. Then Clio opened her purse and started to reload the fish fertilizer and the tools and . . .

"Wait," I said tonelessly. I went inside and returned a moment later with a set of keys. "Here," I said, dropping them in her hand. I took the sack of manure from her arms.

"All right," Clio said. She put the keys in her pocket. She didn't look at me. "Thanks."

"Think nothing of it."

"Bye then."

When she was almost gone, I called out. "You want a ride?"

"I can walk."

"Bye then."

"Bye."

I watched her disappear around the edge of the court. It was a moment before I went back inside. I put the garden things under the sink.

The apartment echoed. I'd never noticed it before.

I got down on the living room floor and sprawled as far as I could. If you stretched enough, you could touch the furniture on the side of the walls. It made me feel big, but the living room was small.

I thought of Pete. If he ever got down on the floor, he

probably did exercises. Not a wasted moment. Mr. Efficiency. I could be like Pete. I summoned my strength, rolled over onto my side, lowered the stylus, rolled back. One economical motion.

I glanced at the score Clio had pulled out of my bookcase, but I soon let it drop. Pre-tilapia Joe played. Post-tilapia Joe felt.

Two-Part Inventions. Bach had it figured out, the relentless procession of tints, the two voices distinct. I concentrated on the bass, the left hand—the offhand in other hands. Both my hands twitched, but I contained them.

I stayed on the floor for the better part of two hours, playing at my most efficient. Only my neurons worked. From time to time I laughed out loud—at a sudden volume, the pindrop end of a technical feat, the spot where Glenn Gould would suppress a fit. No wonder he was good at playing Bach. For the most part, though, I simply absorbed the spare, the spaces between, and breathed the vacant living room air.

Afterward I had a shot of coffee, got out the broom and dust rag and cleaned up the place.

She hadn't picked up after herself, not that I would've liked that, but anyway there it was: the pile of dishes on the table, the dried dollop of toothpaste in the bathroom sink. I made the bed, smoothing the depressions where we'd lain, sliding my hand across the used sheets.

She'd left Aldo's cuttings on the windowsill over the kitchen sink. She'd found a grotty glass somewhere. The ants had found it, too. A line of them marched up and down the side of the glass, taking their turn at the well. I had to clean them up too.

Around six I went to the park. I had planned on walking clear around the lake, but the paths were clogged with baby strollers so I sat down on the grass instead and drank a beer out of a paper bag and watched the sky fog up. When a couple of teenagers shook out a blanket next to me and started to hump, I went back home and made dinner. A peanut butter sandwich was all. We'd had the eggs for brunch.

Before I turned in I threw my sweater over my pyjamas and took my last beer out to the front steps. The court was emptied and quiet, muffled under what was now a thick blanket of fog. George had gone to bed long ago; Suzette's lights were off. Number 4 was up. His TV cast a pale square of light on Clio's garden bed. His cat was up, too, at its post, silhouetted against the TV screen. It was looking at Clio's dirt like it'd been looking all day yesterday and today. As far as I knew, it had never been outside and didn't know dirt from kitty litter.

It was sad, but it was none of my business.

I took a long pull of my beer, felt it slide down my throat. The fog had suspended the scent of that night-flowering tree in a hundred thousand water drops. Victorian Box: now I had the name for it. I guessed that was good. There was another scent, too, in the air. A new one, or actually an old one known to long-ago Joe: the smell of fresh-turned and watered dirt.

Clio's garden plot.

Maybe there were angleworms in there, too, dormant all these years.

Seventeen

"It's Clio, right? Am I right? Don't think I haven't noticed. It's account of Clio you don't have time for me anymore."

"I'm behind in all my work," I told Willy as evenly as I could. "I'm sorry. I'll get to Corazon this afternoon. Right now, if you'll excuse me, I've got a speech to write."

"You're an item, aren't you."

"Leave my personal life out of this," I said, voice rising. "You don't like the way I operate, go find somebody else to do your dirty work. Go ahead! Go!" He squirmed on his own hook, then he left. Fat chance he'd even try. I was one in a million.

Afterward, though, I regretted it. Willy and his libido were supporting Joe's Word. What if he decided to retire? No perks. No pleasure. I'd be writing speeches for Elk Club picnics from now to Armaggedon.

Most of the time during the week I didn't even know when she'd been by. The signs were there, though, if you knew where to look. The garden was getting hoed and weeded, a resurgence of Bermuda grass had been stayed, and the lavender cuttings that had swallowed the glass of water with its tangle of white roots were now settled in the ground beneath the bedroom window. They were filling out fast—all the plants were—as though in payback to Clio's ministries.

It wasn't just in the garden bed that Clio was spending time. I was waking up alongside her on a regular weekend basis these days, and sometimes during the week.

Like this morning. There she was again, mouth open, softly snoring. The sleep of the righteous, of those who have put in quality time with bugs and buds and dirt. She'd thrown off the sheets around her and was bared to the waist. I would let her sleep. I would get up and go off to work and be conscientious for a change. I would just look at her for a while, study her and the hold she had on me.

The pale beauty of her skin. I think that was it. Not the pale of hard china with its brilliant cold finish, but a pale with the kind of luster you see in old stoneware.

That was it. The cream of an old stoneware coffee cup, the kind you held in the palm of your hand warmed with heat slowly released. The curve of her shoulder, the long line of her neck: they were lovely to look at, but it was the flesh you wanted to press.

She lay beside me, a creamy log of flesh.

Through the open window came the rustle of mourning doves in the avocado tree.

I reached over and brushed her arm with my fingertips. "It's late, Clio," I whispered. "Are you awake?"

"No," she said.

That was good enough for me. I moved close, swung my arm around her waist, and not long after, through various deft fleshy maneuvers, I got her to percolate and then there we were again, all limbs and tumble and me pouring cream in her cup.

I must've passed it three or four times before I noticed. The glass that'd housed the lavender roots now held a bouquet of yellow flowers held high on wiry stems. Light from the kitchen window behind it upped the wattage, gave it a halo. I don't know how I'd missed it before. Every time I crossed the apartment—front door to bedroom, living room to head—I crossed its electric beam.

On the second day I moved it over an inch.

On the third day I changed its water.

She brought over some of her records. She wanted to put some juice in my veins—"Get loose!" was her cry—and I liked the music by the old hopheads, but I couldn't stomach some of her contemporary groups. You'd have thought she had enough howling dogs with Mrs. Barry's pack.

As for those hill hounds, her portraits were going well, Clio said. She'd finished four of the six so far and Mrs. Barry had picked out the frames.

The Barrys were giving a big party. We were both invited but I told Clio to count me out. I wasn't much for entertainment. Clio didn't like that side of me. She'd tried to get me to a movie about cockfighters once and she'd lost that bout, but she hadn't given up. She announced triumphantly one day that a repertory theater on the Westside was playing the Glenn Gould biopic.

"On the Westside? Forget it." I turned back to my book.

She let me have it then. She called me an old shoe, but what good did that do? I liked old shoes. I'd seen the real thing anyway—or virtually—on TV. Gould was filmed playing Bach fugues and answering the questions of a German critic who conducted the interview from a special-effects window on the top right-hand side of the screen. The result was truly ghoulish—even without my purple pixels. Gould was great, though, exactly as I'd imagined him, all hunched up. And I was to drive twenty miles to see a stand-in?

Oh, we went once or twice to a baseball game and occasionally we shot pool at night, but it was true: mostly in the evenings we holed up at my place and listened to records and read. She brought over a couple of garden books she'd bought and studied them like they were the codes to heaven. I reread Simenon—not the detective books that made him famous, but the novels that made him great. He had codes in his books, too, but they weren't the kinds you could break.

Clio was curious about what she termed my "passion" for Simenon. It wasn't a passion. Everybody digs into one thing or another in their lives; the more you knew, the deeper you dug, it was completely normal. If anything, my collection of Simenon memorabilia was dispassionate—small but choice—the product of a trip to France long ago when I was already an admirer. The photos of Simenon with Gide and Josephine Baker. The old postcards of Liege, Porquerolles, La Rochelle, Fecamp—locales where Simenon either had lived or situated his dark stories. The map of France blown up and framed and marked with red nail polish.

"Have you ever thought of going back to France?" Clio asked me once. "You know, doing a sort of pilgrimage?"

I cringed at her choice of words. "Who has the money?"

"I'd like to go to Europe," she said. She looked at me a beat too long.

I sorted through the mail that had collected on my desk. It was business as usual till I came across an envelope with a Warner Music Group letterhead. It was from Riff. Inside were three fifty-dollar bills, two joints, and a Xeroxed article from a trade magazine. "Warner Hires Five in New Grass Roots Program," it read. A scrawled note was attached. "Thanks a million, man! I've hit the Big Time thanks to your résumé. What a blast! Forever—Riff."

One hundred fifty bucks. I could pay off my bill at Hank's Garage, maybe treat Teresa to something. Let's hear it for hokum.

Just before noon, a woman's head flicked in and out of my front door. A second later the head returned, this time with a body attached.

I got up to offer her a seat but she wouldn't take it.

"I don't know if I should be here," she said, fidgeting. "But I know I need help."

"Maybe I can help you help yourself," I volunteered.

"I'm not . . . I don't think I'm ready yet."

"For what?"

"A new life."

"Are you sure you won't take a chair, Mrs . . . ?"

"I don't want to take your time. I'm not ready yet," she repeated, but she didn't leave. When the pause became painful, she added, "I need a job. I don't know how to go about it."

"I can definitely help you there. I've helped lots of people—with documented success." I pulled out Riff's testimony.

The woman glanced at it, then darted a look at me. Even her eyes wouldn't sit still. "I don't know that a blast is what I need."

"Of course not. I tailor each résumé to match the individual's special character. Just what . . ."

"I've been devastated by my divorce. I can barely get the groceries."

"You've done the right thing by coming here. You need to get out and mingle with other people—if only for your mental health. People need people." I put my hand lightly and for a fraction of a second on her arm. "Coming here was a good start, Mrs. . . ."

"Evans. His name is all I have left. I'm wondering if I should keep it."

"That's one of the things we could talk about if you like, though I believe that's a decision best made on your own. What we mostly need to do is have a nice long chat and find the constructive activities in your background that will appeal to prospective employers."

"I've never had a job before." Her forehead was all furrows.

"How are your computer skills?"

"I can work an electric typewriter—is that okay?" She looked at me. "It's not okay?" She clasped her purse. "I don't know where I'd be without my garden. The Los Angeles River?" she ventured.

"You can always take computer classes, Mrs. Evans, but if you'll excuse me for being so obvious: have you considered a job in gardening?"

"Yes, I have. It's just . . . I haven't been thinking clearly about anything." Another long pause. "It's just a hobby."

"It's not a hobby to the profession. Gardening is big business. Very big business. They need an experienced workforce."

This time her eyes met mine and stayed.

"I'll be honest with you, Mrs. Evans. I'd have to recommend a full-fledged presentation piece. I'm afraid with your . . . maturity, you'll need more than a pro forma résumé. We need to show how your age actually enhances your value to an employer. I'd like you to meet briefly with my art director." I held my breath.

"That sounds expensive."

"You should think of this as an investment. She's also a gardener. You'll like her." I jotted an appointment on my business card and held it out to her. "I marked you down for an interview at this time two weeks from today. I want you to use the intervening period to think positively, okay? I suggest you sit in your garden and observe your plants—not the young ones, not the seedlings full of sap, but the older, established plants that have survived repeated stress over the years, from bug attacks, drought, what have you. The next time we meet you'll be much stronger. You've been through a storm, Mrs. Evans. You've been beaten to the ground, your flowers are heavy with mud. But you're going to lift yourself up and shine again, and you're going to be admired."

"You're quite a talker," she said with a flicker of amusement. She looked twenty years younger.

"You keep your end of the bargain by showing up, and I'll keep mine. We'll get you a job."

"I believe you, Mr. . . ." She looked at my card.

"Just call me Joe."

Little by little pieces of Clio accumulated in the apartment like dust motes you don't even notice till one day the sun hits them right. The garden books, the toiletries in the oversized kit, the spare outfit in the closet. I think it really hit home, though, the night of the car accident down the street.

We both woke bolt upright. A long awful silence: had we dreamed it? Then the screeching tires, the siren, the whop of helicopters and police in pursuit.

Clio jumped out of bed.

I lurched at her. "Stay inside!" I yelled.

"Are you crazy? Of course I will!" She was staring at me, bug-eyed, in the streaming white light. "I was just going to the bathroom to get my toilet kit. I'm pretty sure I've got an extra pair of earplugs there."

Suzette was at an audition, George and Sargent were off to Griffith Park. There were just the two of us — Number 4's cat and I — watching Clio get a grip on her favorite plant.

Drawing felicia. She worked in charcoal.

"Your garden looks great," I said and I meant it. "It's really filling up."

Clio's gaze skipped back and forth from flower to paper. "The closer plants are, the happier they are."

"Is that so."

"You never noticed how plants at the edge of cornfields are puny compared to the rest? That's 'cause they're not surrounded by the others. They have no buffer between themselves and the world. It's the same thing with a plant all alone in a garden bed. It may survive, but it'll never thrive. Plants like company."

She picked up a chamois to work a smudge.

"What about in the desert?" I said. "Plants in the desert live far apart."

Clio gave me a dirty look and switched subjects. "I usually don't care for daisy-type flowers, but I've fallen for this one. It's really resilient." She paused. "It comes from South Africa, the Cape of Good Hope."

"Where they have all the storms?"

"It's rare to have blue flowers in the garden — and such modest ones, too, not like those gross petunias that got wiped out by the caterpillars." A second later she said, "You know that bug spray I got at the nursery? That Bt thing Beanie's always talking about? I asked him some more about it. He says it's toxic to all sorts of caterpillars, and butterflies by extension. It's being genetically engineered, too — into our food crops — with a bacteria as a vector that's considered the cancer of the plant world."

"Don't go Beanie on me, Clio."

"And they call it a natural pesticide. . . . The EPA says it's safe, but how can they know what could happen twenty years down the road?"

"Better stop, Clio. It'll drive you crazy."

"I suppose you're right," she sighed. "What can you do?"

"Draw felicias."

"You know what I'd really like to do? Grow plants from seed. It takes time and commitment, but it's much more satisfying in the end."

"I wouldn't bother," I said.

Clio had placed a couple of Beanie's pinwheels in each corner of the garden bed to scare off the squirrels. The plastic rotated slowly as the day warmed, catching the first currents of air that breezed through the court. They made a dry clicking sound, like distant castanets.

"Did you ever get any feedback on that résumé I did?" Clio asked.

"Yes, I did. Riff got a job with a record company. A good one."

"You might have told me." She sounded peeved.

"I just did."

Clio's frown deepened. "Any new business along those lines?" she said, trying to keep her tone even.

"Maybe."

She waited but nothing else came. "Well then," she said in exasperation, "if you have and I can help, I'd like to become involved earlier and work together like a copywriter and art director, you know? That way you can do a résumé justice."

"I'm operating a business, Clio. It has nothing to do with justice."

"But I know I can make a difference down the road. We can build up that side of your operations."

The pinwheels were clattering now. They were getting on my nerves. "Look, Clio, I'm already paying you peanuts and I can't—I won't—pay you any more."

"Well, that's all right. I'd still do it."

"Why?" I said. Now I was peeved. "You enjoy being a carpet?"

She looked shocked. "Is that how you see it?" The morning was successfully breaking apart. "Haven't you ever heard of spec?"

"Yeah, I've heard of spec. It's the sort of thing you do when you're desperate."

"It's the sort of thing you do when you care," she exploded.

"All right," I announced. "I'm going inside. Maybe now you can make some headway on your art."

She said it under her breath, in a voice smooth as sandpaper: "What's the matter? Afraid I'll walk on your willy?"

If she pretended not to say it, I pretended not to hear it.

When I came out a half-hour later, she was gone and the steps of the stoop were covered with charcoal fingerprints.

Usually it was enough to sweep them out the door. You knew they'd be back, but you also knew they'd get the message eventually, alerted by signals sent from the maimed, their little feelers twitching. Sometimes they got the better of you and then you had to get them where they lived, following their trail back to a crack in the concrete or a hummock of soil, then pouring in a kettle of boiling water. It was better than arsenic, but it wasn't surefire. Maybe you weakened them and they died later. Maybe deep inside the nest you got their eggs.

The last time I'd poured boiling water in the ground it'd seeped over into the new felicias. I'd picked up a tree branch and scratched the soil near their limp stems. I'd hoped Clio would take me for a squirrel.

"I told you: I'm not going and that's that. I don't care for parties and I don't care for her. She doesn't want me anyway, she's just being polite. And she just wants you because you're young and pretty. You're part of her decor . . ."

A light plane buzzed overhead, trailing a gauzy billboard. We barely gave it a glance. We were pumping the Funboat pedals like mad, venting steam.

"That's not true. She wants me because she thinks I'm an artist. Plus I'm not that young anymore." Then she added, defiantly, "She says she's going to introduce me around."

"To dog society? So you can do more dog portraits?"

"So what's wrong with that? You're telling me your clients are more noble?" I swung the steering wheel suddenly to the left and for a second we got doused by the water fountain's drift. I was sure of it now. Teresa had told her about Willy. But how much?

"Can't we just enjoy ourselves, Clio, and take in the sun?" I said a moment later. "Let's just close our eyes and pretend we're out pedaling in Interlachen, or Lake Como or Lac Lamans."

"Of course," Clio murmured. She shook her head like a dog, spraying me with water a second time, and then we floated around Lac Echo Park with our eyes shut and hung our thoughts out on the line to dry. When we opened our eyes again we found we had drifted straight toward the concrete banks and a band of angry fishermen.

"What on earth do they fish here?" Clio said as we pedaled back to the center. "Do they actually eat what they catch? This place is a sewer."

"Wrong," I said with authority, for I'd done a job once for an employee of the Urban Fishery Program. "Echo Park Lake has spring water as a source."

"And the other source is a sewer."

"The Fish and Game Department stocks fish. There's even a kid's fishing program called *Los Tiburones*—The Sharks. If you want to catch kids these days, you don't call it The Tadpoles."

"So what do they stock—shark?"

"Trout and catfish. The ones that survive turn dark and dull. The experts say they're safe enough to eat. There's also some tilapia and a few goldfish and carp."

"It's too romantic," Clio said, trailing her hand in the inky water. "An inner-city lake teeming with dull, dark survivors. How come they have to be dull—can't they just be dark?"

"There's eel here, too."

Clio retrieved her hand.

Our hour was almost over and our thighs were getting

tired. We figured we had time, though, to pedal by the lotus beds. The Echo Park Lotus Festival was coming up. Clio was sure by now the plants would be in bud.

The foliage was lush, saturated green, straight from the realm of Tarzan. Giant pads rose heavily three and four feet into the air. Here and there spikes carrying fat buds towered above the rest. One of them had speared a plastic grocery bag on its way up; it waved its flag over the surrounding lotus beds, announcing great values.

Behind the lotus bed was the curved white facade of the Church of the Four Square Gospel. We looked for Mrs. Ellroy—there was always a chance she'd be hobbling by. Instead we saw Beanie walking down Glendale. We waved but he didn't see us. We were starting to turn the boat around when we saw the first stone hit. Beanie looked up in the sky, startled. He got the next one square in the back and this one seemed to register. Still he didn't look back, even when the kids were pelting him at a steady pitch. Clio and I yelled and waved our arms but there was nothing we could do. We sat still on the water for a moment. No one likes to see these things.

Then we realized we had to cross the whole lake in eight minutes or get charged an extra hour.

We ground our thighs to the task. The wake churned behind us but there was a head wind and progress was slow. At one point we started to laugh, it was so silly, but then we pumped harder and saved our breath.

Ten yards out from the dock we saw we were going to make it. We coasted in on our momentum with one minute

to spare. That moment—a moment of pure athletic tri-
umph—was when Clio chose to mention the dog party
again.

"Christ, Clio! I told you: go on your own! Do you need
me to go everywhere with you?"

The Funboat assistants reached out to guide us in.

"This isn't 'everywhere.' I've never asked you to a party
before."

"Don't you get it? Do I have to spell it out?"

The boat hands exchanged glances, did their rope thing.

She kept her voice low. Real low, just for me. "We're a
couple when we go to baseball games. We're a couple at
the Short Stop. . . ." She lowered her voice even further.
". . . We're a couple when it comes to bed. . . ." She bounded
suddenly onto the dock. The hired hands jumped to stabilize
the boat. For a few crazy seconds, it looked like I was going
to capsize.

She was yards away when I reached the shore and she
wasn't stopping. "I thought you liked baseball games!" I
called out to her back.

Eighteen

The gates creaked open and we rolled through. Inside, the drive was dark as night except where bands of moonlight fell from cracks between the trees. Clio's nail polish reflected the light, on and off, on and off in the next seat.

Nail polish. That was new.

I don't know where she'd gotten her dress. It seemed to have been fashioned from inner tubing.

At the colonnade all was light and action. We were greeted by a pack of valets. I handed my keys to one young man who passed them on to a subordinate who passed them on to a lackey who slumped into my dump and made it vanish.

No sign of the dogs; I hoped they'd been put to sleep.

From somewhere below came the boom of a band. Below was where the house was, too, down a switchbacked flight of steps. The shrubbery that lined the approach was littered with plastic champagne glasses.

June Barry met us at the teak-slabbed door. "Clio and Joe! How nice of you both to come. Art," she called behind her. "Clio and her man are here."

"Who?" a voice sounded from another room.

"Clio and her man."

A moment later Art appeared — younger than he appeared on TV, but then tonight he wasn't wearing as much makeup.

"Joe is the writer I was telling you about, remember?" June said to Art as she introduced us. "Joe likes his scotch on the rocks." She gave me a sly smile, then turned to the next group of arrivals.

Art clasped my shoulder. "I like a man with style. C'mon, Joe, let me show you the way to the bar. We've invited another writer tonight, I'd like you to meet him. He's around here somewhere." Art took us through a hall hewn directly from hillside rock. It opened unexpectedly onto an Olympic-sized room with views of the lawn, the party in progress and the L.A. basin spread out below. "There he is!" he said, pointing to a figure standing just outside the door. An instant later he'd fetched him.

"Joe, this is Bill Harding; Bill, this is Joe . . . what did you say your name was?" The conversation stalled before it had even started. "You're both writers," Art said to us in mock exasperation. "See if you can come up with some dialogue." He excused himself and left. He hadn't introduced Clio. She looked pissed.

Bill Harding looked at me dully, sizing me up. "So, Joe . . . what are your credits? Anything produced?"

"I'm not that kind of writer," I said.

"Don't tell me you're a real writer."

"You can't get more real."

There was a silence to fill when I wouldn't elaborate.

"I write novelizations myself," the guy said finally. He stood his ground.

"I'd love to hear all about it, Bill," I said, delivering my exit lines. "Can I get back to you? You know how it is with writers: I've got to hit the bar."

He seemed relieved. "Absolutely! Duty first!" he urged.

"Sorry," Clio mustered as we stepped out onto the lawn—or rather I stepped and Clio stumbled. She was wearing a new pair of shoes, too. The heels were shaped like golf tees.

"It's nothing," I said. "Nothing that a double scotch won't cure."

The bodies at the bar were six deep, and I had to elbow my way through twice to get my double. Clio seemed perturbed that I was actually drinking scotch. She was thinking maybe I was going to get drunk and cause a scene?

I loosened up some when the liquor hit. Clio and I pointed out to each other various over-the-top hairdos. It was too bad Teresa hadn't been invited; she'd have been thrilled. One woman's hair was lacquered and woven into a provincial market basket. Inside were wild strawberries.

I leaned over and paid Clio a compliment. It wasn't me talking, it was the liquor, but it was what she'd been waiting for all evening long and she drank it in. Her eyes sparkled. I bent back to my scotch.

"Clio! Joe! What are you doing?" June Barry was upon us. "Don't you know the first thing about party protocol? You're supposed to cir-cu-late. Clio, I want you to meet Bob and Eileen Ferguson. I've told them about you." She started to lead Clio away.

"Aren't you coming?" Clio asked.

"You have your fun," I told her. She seemed to be enjoying the attention.

I pushed my way back to the bar, and when I reemerged Clio was off by the swimming pool surrounded by toupees and weather forecasters and cumulus cloud hairdos. She scanned the crowd once as if looking for me. She went at it wrong. She should've known where I'd be.

I looked down at my drink—my third or fourth? I was getting sloshed.

Liquified, watered down, soggy greenbacked lawn.

Where were the dogs?

I walked carefully toward the house. Should get something to eat. Something solid. Dog food. I took a short cut through some bushes and flushed out a couple of clipped turkeys. The guests loved it. They pointed first at me and then at the speeding, zigzagging birds. A few people applauded.

Get me outta here.

I ducked into an open door and found myself in a long, dark corridor. At the end, bright lights and a dull roar. Food, I thought, moving toward the light. I emerged into a sort of atrium surrounding a shallow pool. I was right on the money: under the arcades were a series of banquet tables loaded with pyramids of glistening meats. There was a crush of guests here, too. And there were the dogs Clio had told me about—the Bernese Mountain, Afghan, Bullmastiff and Briard, the Bouvier des Flandres, and the hot Spinone. I flinched at the sight, but they weren't interested in me, or anyone else for that matter. They were too busy dragging roast beef off the tables and vacuuming up spilled capon salad. Someone nearby exclaimed at the sight, but another pointed out there was plenty of food to go around.

The few couches scattered here and there were squatted by the dogs now, full of roast beef, digesting. "It's not their fault," a fellow guest explained when she saw my expression. "We're the intruders here. This is their exercise room when it rains."

I found a slab of meat that hadn't been mauled and carried it back outside, and when I spotted Clio again she was on the far side of the lawn near the gazebo, cir-cu-lating with her old friend the sculptor. My. What a smart party. Not one, but two artists. He was wearing the same paint-splattered T-shirt, the walking billboard featuring his big barrel chest. He probably didn't wash the one or the other in order to preserve his *essence d'ennui*.

I turned around and took another stab at my meat.

The band was playing a medley of Beatles' songs. Wave after wave of contorted sound passed over my head. I couldn't stand it anymore. I lurched toward the house and on the third try found an empty room. Looked like it was the dogs' mess hall. It'd barely had time to register when I realized I wasn't so alone after all. June Barry had followed me in.

"Here you are. I've been looking for you all evening," she said. "Who are you hiding from?"

"The life force."

"Why Joe. You've been drinking," she said with amusement. She came up close.

"I suppose this is about your husband?" I asked.

"Of course it is. You know I want you to write his book. From what Clio tells me, it'd be a change from your normal work, you might enjoy it. I can give you a long lead time. It's a memoir, after all, there's nothing urgent—unless he loses his memory," she laughed.

She stepped closer still, rubbed right up against my privacy bubble. Her outfit tonight was elegant, restrained. Only her hair hung loose.

"I could help you with the material, you know," she said, lowering her voice, looking up through her lashes. Her gaze was steady, confident. And why not? She was as good as money could get.

"You're just bored," I said.

She laughed. "See? I knew you were right for Art's book."

I didn't follow the logic, but what I did see—with clarity—was that while she was ticking off various other incentives, she was starting to play with one of my shirt buttons. And I was letting her do it.

"We could have fun," she said.

It was crazy. I was already up to my ears in sex at work and now sex at home. All I needed was more sex on the side. But that was the thing about hormones. When you're running around half-cocked all the time, it doesn't take much to set you off.

Certainly a lot less than a pair of lips brushed against your neck. "Don't say no," she murmured.

"No," I said. And then I pulled her against me and came down on her mouth.

I was one of her dogs, wasn't I. She was wanting to pump

my sperm and here I was wanting to oblige her. Who knows what might've happened—she wasn't taking my no for an answer—if she hadn't peeled herself away.

"I've got to get back to my other guests," she said, rearranging her dress, smoothing her hair.

I drew my hand across my mouth. "Is this how you interview your other writers?" I asked.

"There is no other," she said in a low voice, coming up close again, the time it took to slide a calling card into my shirt pocket. "You're the man for the job." Then she walked out.

I stood there for a couple of minutes, just stood there in the center of the room. I looked around again. I wanted to remember. The single chair, the sink, the mop. The row of stainless steel bowls on the cement floor for the dogs' food and water. And on the wall, above each set of serving dishes: Clio's portraits. Shamus. Rockwell. The four others. My gaze traveled from one to the other.

I picked up the glass of wine I'd set on the floor. I tossed it back in one swallow and stumbled outdoors. To the left was the party, the lights, the music, the noise. I turned right, into the dark.

I walked till the landscape got rough and the lawn gave out and before me was the ten-foot wall of the estate. The dividing line. On the one side the dreamers, the dreamers of one-man shows, of owning a house, of paying off credit cards. On the other, the ones who lived their dreams and lived in fear of losing them. I looked back at the huge hothouse, heard the muffled sounds of booze and band. Art and June Barry, stockholders in the dream factory.

"I've got a ticket to ride!" I wailed.

I wanted to see. I wanted to be above.

I started to climb a nearby tree. I lost my footing and one of my shoes and had to scramble to get up onto a limb overhanging the wall. I straddled it for a moment while I caught my breath. I could see now. I could see the lights of L.A. glinting between the twigs and branches. Where were the fireflies? I wanted to see the fireflies. I inched my way out on the limb, pulled back the foliage.

Fireflies in paradise. Hundreds of thousands of tinkerbells rising from the land at twilight. Hundreds of thousands of tinkerbells snuffed by the Peace Corps. I blinked back the wet, just a liquor wet, blinked back the dozens of fireflies flying through the skies. Glowing fireflies. With nasty whirling blades. Tinkerbells from hell.

Fucking branches! I couldn't see.

I jumped off the tree onto the wall. Now I could see.

Now everyone could see. Some mechanism had been triggered somewhere and suddenly I was blinded by floodlights. Sirens blasted the air, mockingbirds shrieked. Back in the manor, dogs dropped their roast beef on the atrium floor and sprang through the door and raced across the lawn, followed by streams of partygoers trailing marijuana smoke, secure in their numbers, curious to see what had got trapped by the yelping pack.

They were all white through the floodlights. I couldn't make out their faces, they were all washed white by the light. Lots of little gnats.

Somewhere out there would be Clio.

Nineteen

"This a new brand of coffee, Teresa?"

"No, it's the same old same old. Why? Does it taste funny?"

I gave my head a shake and poured more cream in my cup just as Gloria walked in the door. "Yuck. It's a stew out there. Hi, Mom. Hey, Slim!" she called out to me. "Long time no see. What'cha been up to?"

"He tied one on the other night," Teresa answered for me. "Speaking of which, Joe," she continued, "where's Clio? I haven't seen her all week."

"She's coming in today," I said. It came out strained.

Gloria noticed. She smiled sweetly at me. "I hear the two of you are a number." Then, with impeccable timing: "Would that be absolute? Or divisible." She burst out laughing.

It wasn't her fault. She was still a girl.

I took my coffee over to a seat next to Willy. "She wants more money," I whispered. "Photos. We're in like Flynn."

"Who does," he whispered back.

"Corazon."

Teresa wagged a rat-tail in our direction. "Speak up, boys. No secrets here. You want secrets, you step next door."

"We're talking baseball."

"My eye."

"More money? Sure, why not," Willy said. "Can't take it to heaven with me, can I?"

"Heaven?" I said, getting up.

Teresa tapped the swivel chair. "Gloria dear, come over here. Be good to your mother. Let me give you a brioche."

"Oh Mom, puh-lease. That style's so *passé.*"

"How could it be? It isn't even out yet—it was just in a pilot last week."

Gloria rolled her eyes. "Haven't you ever heard of *pre*-TV? Take a look at the streets, for heaven's sake. That's where it's at."

You could take a look at Gloria while you were at it. She amazed me, she was so out of step with other kids her age. Hardworking, family-oriented. No "Vida Loca" for her.

"They're mostly wearing Shannas here," Teresa mused. "Except for Clio, of course."

"Clio, Clio, Clio. Wake up, Mom. She's . . . what?" Gloria looked at me, ". . . fifty?"

"She's thirty-five, isn't that right, Joe?" Teresa said. "And she's one breath of fresh air. In fact, I've been thinking of taking a picture of her and putting it in the window. She's my showcase, after all. What d'ya think, Joe? Maybe even have it done up professional, a nice big photo so everyone walking down the street can see my work."

"A pedestrian got run down on Glendale this morning," I said.

"Another? Where? Dead down?"

"In the bag, on the crosswalk under Sunset. I saw the Beamer who did it. He didn't look too happy."

"Not too happy," Willy said. "He'll be late for work."

Gloria called out from behind the partition where she was sorting towels. "You need to change the Roach Motel again, Mom."

"Why not just put a pigeon back there," I suggested.

"They eat cockroaches?" Teresa said amiably, bending back to her latest project, installing a display case in the storefront window. I watched as she fiddled with the screws and pliers and metal parts. She seemed to have been energized by the piñata I'd bought her. New piñata. New display case. Espresso machine. Promo with Clio. Teresa was running on optimism, racking up her dreams.

Promo of Clio. Two feet high.

I washed out my cup and went next door. I had a lot of work piled up. I'd had to lay low for two days following the dog party and even now the memory of the night made me burp.

With a little discipline, though, I could catch up. Aldo, for one, would be fairly easy, and I'd pretty much finished with Mrs. Evans. Corazon was more problematic. And Natasha— well, I'd have to put her off again. I needed sap for that, and for a week now I hadn't been able to get it up.

I got started on Aldo. He'd managed to get a snapshot of one of the car repair customers passing cash to a big bicep. There'd been more plant damage, too, and he'd recorded that. I held up the photo and studied it. Another rabbit ear missing.

After the letter to Sergeant Ramsey, there was the backup

to the 13th Council District. Councilwoman Hasfeld had been booted out in the June elections and a new councilman put in place. Naturally, our file hadn't been transferred. I had to review the situation and make copies of every last piece of scrap. It was a fun morning. It was almost a relief when Clio turned up.

Almost.

She was dabbing at her nose.

"You too?" I asked.

She nodded. "It's early this year."

She sat down opposite and looked at me across the desk with her nougat eyes.

We hadn't seen each other since the dog party. She'd called me once. We'd talked about this and that, mostly about my hangover. I didn't mention her dog portraits, she hadn't mentioned her Ennui. We'd both skirted the wall.

"I watered your garden this morning," I said.

"You didn't need to. The plants can take a drought."

"They looked better after."

"Thanks."

"Want a cup of coffee?"

"No, let's get going." She pulled out her sketch pad.

I flopped Mrs. Evans' file onto the desk. "She's going to try for assistant manager of an upscale nursery," I said. "She's educated, articulate, sensitive. She's been traumatized by a divorce to the point of timidity, but I think it's fleeting. She strikes me as a wise old woman."

Clio glanced at the data I'd typed up. "She's only fifty-eight," she laughed.

"We play up the maturity angle, make it a positive. You can hire kids to lug pots, and computers can get information, but she's got forty-five years of gardening experience and that doesn't grow on trees. You'll see that I emphasized that in my personal statement: forty-five years of playing in dirt."

"That's a lot of hands on."

"Her grandfather owned a small nursery in the valley before the depression; that's where she got the bug. Here, this might interest you: it's a picture of her own garden." I passed the Poloroid across the desk.

A smile spread across Clio's face. "That's wild," she said with admiration.

"That's the word for it. Don't include it in the visual." I got myself a Kleenex and held out the box to Clio, but she'd brought along a pack of her own. "She has a B.A. and speaks Spanish, too," I continued, "which is a major plus, but other than that she has few related accomplishments. She ran the Logan Street Elementary School 'Peter Rabbit' program for a year. They grew vegetables . . ."

"What a strange choice of names. Didn't Peter Rabbit get killed by the old lady?"

"I don't remember; Beanie would know . . . And just recently she held the position of assistant director of the Echo Park Beautification Project. That's about it. It's not much." I gathered all the material together, including my meeting notes and my personal statement and handed over Mrs. Evans to Clio. "Got any questions?"

Clio dithered with her pencil for a moment. I watched her breasts breathe under the weave of her dress.

"Yes," she said. "What's the Echo Park Beautification Project?"

I shrugged. "She advises her neighbors."

"And you were the director?"

"She needed a reference."

Clio got up with a sigh, stuffed her sketchbook and Mrs. Evans' file into her purse, and flung the bag over her shoulder. She had to take a step backward to recover her balance. She was wearing a pair of barely-there sandals with pearls at the thongs. "The Lotus Festival starts tonight," she said, trying hard to sound offhand.

"Yeah, I've seen the banners."

"I've decided to do a series on lotus blooms. If they're any good, I'm going to send them around. I'm determined not to give up." She gave a little laugh. "The lotus bud is said to ressemble the shape of hands in prayer."

"Will you be praying in charcoal?"

She shook her head. "Pen and ink. Charcoal is the obvious choice because the flower is so voluptuous, but I want to play against that." She adjusted the strap of her purse a millimeter. "The festival is staying open till nine tonight. Wanna go after work?"

"Tonight? No, I can't. I'm sorry."

"No big deal. It's going on all weekend long."

When you're taking half-steps, it takes time to exit a room. I looked down at her exposed baby toes.

"Wait," I said, and she stopped fast. I reached into my desk drawer and pulled out an envelope. "I almost forgot. These are seeds from Mrs. Evans' garden. She wanted you to have them."

She murmured her thanks; they trailed her out the door.

Seconds later, Rock 'n' Roll Riff appeared at the door.

"Watta chick!" he exclaimed, staring after her as he gave my hand a shake. He ignored my bleat of pain. He was busy cruising the streets of Beverly Hills with Clio, looking for pizza. "What's she doing with you?"

"She's my art director," I said, massaging my knuckles.

"Your art director? What a gas! Was she the one who did my résumé? I don't suppose you could introduce me?" Then he saw something in my eyes that made him reflect. I didn't think he had it in him. "You two aren't . . . are you?" He did the thing with his fingers they do on TV.

"What can I do for you, Riff?" I asked.

He gave me a broad smile. He'd had his teeth bonded. "Did you get my announcement?" he asked.

"Of course. Congratulations. And thanks for the enclosures. That was white of you."

"Nah, it was just good business. You have to spend money to make money, everyone knows that."

"What else do you know?"

"That I have to write my first report for the Grass Roots Program and it's due in two weeks." He picked up his briefcase, it was made of the kind of leather that was massaged three times a day when it was still alive, and pulled out a stack of crisp greens. "Your retainer," he said, waving it at me. Then he pulled out a pile of documents, everything he said I could possibly need to write "The Psychographic Profile of the Eighteen- to Thirty Year-Old White Male CD Consumer in Contemporary Urban Markets."

"You're kidding," I said glumly.

He pointed to one of the papers. "This is a study they did last year on aging white males. Just include the new data and rewrite the conclusion. Relax, don't worry about it. No one ever acts on these things. It's just busywork for juniors."

He snapped shut his briefcase. "I gotta dash. I'm off to Palm Springs for a few days. Can it be ready a week from Tuesday on disc? Great. And listen, man: can you throw in a couple jokes at the beginning? Something wild and crazy— like in my résumé?"

After he left I thumbed through the papers and pulled out one that was headlined "Brief Capsules of the VALS Types." It seemed there were three types in this world: Need Driven, Outer Directed, and Inner Directed, with subsections further categorizing the concepts. I scanned one of them:

> * *I-Am-Me's* (4%) This is a young, narcissistic, and fiercely individualistic group, for whom whim and the mood of the moment are the key lifestyle imperatives. Not surprisingly, their individualism often smacks of peer-group trendiness. In many ways, I-Am-Me-ness is a transitional phase from Outer Directedness to Inner Directedness.

All the categories were of this order, about as fun and scientific as one of Teresa's hairdo magazine quizzes. Was Mrs. Evans an Experiential? Teresa an Emulator? What about Clio? Who was Joe?

Joe didn't seem to fit.

I took an early lunch and a handi-pak of Kleenex along for company.

As I headed to the Brite Spot, the air was smoggy, stagnant. The white light of pollution, diffused, pointillist. If French impressionists were painting today, I thought to myself as I trudged up the street, they'd flock to Echo Park as they once did to Normandy in order to capture the light.

Mornings were the worst. By early afternoon better air would blow in from the Westside, once residents there had finished with it.

Back at my desk I got going on Corazon. In the new photo she'd sent she was lying curled on top of a bed as if taking a siesta, the pleats of her schoolgirl skirt jacked high to her thighs. One of her kneesocks lay rumpled down around her ankle.

I propped the photo beside me and, with one eye on the thigh, I reread her letter.

Dear Daddy,

You see how easy it is to call you Daddy, Daddy? Already I feel we so closer now. Thank you so much for your long letters and how you open to me. I feel it is a gift and maybe a road to what they call love.

There it is — I say the word on paper now. But is it wrong to maybe love the one I call Daddy?

Thank you for money order too. That really help me till I find another job. I promise I buy lots of food so I be your round baby like in the photograph. A friend takes this picture when I am asleep, and I think maybe it is good you see it because I think it is when we are asleep that our insides show. You know what I mean?

The person who is taking this picture says I am good to the

eyes when I sleep. He says he wants to take more pictures of
me, but I don't think he has dollars to pay for film. It must be
A-okay to live in Los Angeles in the middle of Hollywood and
all the stars. Do you ever write for the movie? You can write a
movie from your book about the car theives catched in a web
of desire. My favorite star is Sylvester Stallone. You look like
him if you ate more. You have same sad eyes.

Remember those exercises you tell me to do when I feel
sad and all alone that start with my belly button? They make
me feel funny inside like when I see Sylvester Stallone. The last
time I do the rub I go below where you tell me to go, and it is
just like you are telling me. The bell is strong and shake me up
and then I sleep and sleep. You say this is what love is, to love
yourself first, but this is hard for me because ever since I am
little girl I am teaching to put other first. Still I wonder about
the other love, like in the movies with a man and a woman.
I wish you are here. I am so lonely now and have no one to
teach me the ways of life and love. Young men come to me
and I know they want to be with me like in the movies, but
they push in my face and have fat wet lips. I going to love
myself every night now, and sleep so good, but I wish I was
with my Daddy and can learn how to love on his lap.

I know I must not wish too hard, but I feel more and more
like we are like mud and lightening and one day we going to
connect.

> Good night sweet Daddy,
> your baby girl Corazon

I got out Willy's stationery and the pen with the thick nib.
A wisp of air from the open window curled down my neck.
I turned on the fan, pushed it in my face.

Fat wet lips.

My dear Corazon,

I am completely charmed by the photograph you have sent and deeply appreciate your sharing this moment of intimacy. It is as though I've peeked into the bedroom of my own daughter (if I'd had one). I can certainly understand why your friend wants to take more pictures, especially at this stage in your life when you are at your most vulnerable, no longer a child, not yet a woman. It would be my privilege to pay for film for your friend. Although he has yet to master his technical skills, he shows signs of being an artist himself. Not everyone can capture the *tristesse d'innocence* as he has. I enclose a money order to cover the costs of his time and materials and ask only that you send me copies of the pictures so that I can share being there.

Perhaps you could also send along a picture of your friend. Is he a young man himself?

I enjoyed your observation, Corazon, about the transparency of our inner nature. The more we correspond, the more you reveal yourself a remarkably sensitive young woman. I would love to be able to see you and discuss such things, and I am convinced that this will happen. I want to believe that one day I will hold you in my arms and help guide you through the weightier aspects of life that worry you, such as the man/woman thing.

I can tell you this much, though, Corazon: that the rapport between a man and woman can be exquisite if approached in a mature and sensitive fashion. At the summit of this rapport is the act of love itself, of moving and rubbing together. There is nothing better than the act of love as an expression of mutual respect—consumed by passion, yes, but tempered with tenderness. This is the union I have been seeking all these lonely years, the perfect union with the other.

You are right, Corazon, to push away the young men who violate your space. They are only after their immediate pleasure; they don't understand that the one thing that can help them achieve the most exquisitely expansive and lasting of pleasures is a sense of partnership and reciprocity. This is something that only a mature man like myself can come to appreciate; that, plus a knowledge that a woman has the right to a room of her own. If a gentleman hopes to find his pleasure in her room, he must never force the door with a coarse and hurried approach, but always ring the doorbell before he enters. If he takes the time to ring the bell, he will find the door wide open.

Now I can hear you say to yourself—I can hear you as clearly as if you were sitting across from me at the breakfast table: "This guy Will, he is so full of abstractions! I want to know what love is in the flesh and bone." And so I will give you a little idea of what man's love is like when it comes knocking at your door:

You know the actor you mentioned in your letter, Sly Stallone? You know his biceps? You know how those biceps look when Sly lifts a submachine gun, how his skin grows taut and swollen with its charge, the veins bulging with tense demand? This is what a man's love looks like, Corazon, when he wants to enter a woman's room. A man's sexual member is a powerful muscle not unlike Sly's biceps that you'd want to stroke and hold—only it is so much better, because a woman, even a small woman, can clasp one hand almost all the way around it while her bell is being rung and lick it like a lollipop.

Love like this is a happy experience that overflows when the couple is finally joined.

Oh, Corazon, this is so tough to talk to you at such a distance. Who knows what will come of all this? All I know is that you are far, far away and I am here in Los Angeles. It is hardest when I am home, thinking of you, watching the shimmer of my garden in the summer heat, the flush of roses and the fat bees that come to visit, drunk with pollen and perfume.

> My dear Corazon, my little love bud,
> Dad

At five o'clock I flipped over the cardboard and closed shop. Beanie walked in at 5:40, late again. On the streets you couldn't own a watch.

I set his monthly check on the desk, plus a pen for his John Hancock. After he'd signed, Arnold E. Turnbull sighed and sat back in his chair. It looked like he was settling in for the winter, which was at least six months off. I didn't know what was up; the check was our only business.

"Can I get you a cup of coffee?" I asked after a couple months had passed.

"Yes, thank you, that would be nice."

I returned a moment later, shutting both the door and the door vent. Teresa had seen Beanie's knees jutting out of the client's chair. She'd have her ears to the crack.

I served Beanie, returned to my seat and waited for him to spill the beans. And waited. And waited.

I've never been much for talk myself, it was just the way I was. I've noticed, though, that it generally gave me the upper hand. People were destabilized by silence; they'd say just

about anything to fill the vacuum and usually it was Grade A
kapok. But I wasn't after power. What good was having the
upper hand unless you wanted to slap people around?

I turned up the force on the fan. The nylon cord, stirred
by the rush of air, clinked at regular intervals against the
metal pole. Next door the dentista was filing down a tooth.

"What's the matter? Membership drive in a dive?" I said at
last, trying to keep it light.

"Sometimes I wonder if I'm making a dent," he nodded.
"God knows I try." He gave the dollar on his beanie a flick. It
twirled for a few seconds before running out of gas.

"You're not making things worse," I offered.

"Tell me what you think. Please."

I stretched my legs under the table, brushed up against
Beanie, pulled them back. "I think a lot of the people you
speak to don't understand English," I said. "Why don't you
learn Spanish? Or try another part of town?"

"In the other parts of town they understand but they
don't listen."

"What good does it do to listen if you can't act on what
you've heard?" He'd asked my opinion. "Knowledge is worse
than ignorance. You get zits from frustration and then your
hair falls out."

I realized Beanie's hair threw my theory back in my face.
Curls sprang out at right angles from the side of his head as
though galvanized by his thoughts. But maybe he'd had elec-
troshock.

"You're wrong there," he countered. "Knowledge is power."

"Knowledge is paralysis," I pooed.

"Not true! Knowledge is the road to revolution!"

It'd been awhile since I'd heard the word. "Then it's a dead end," I laughed. "Who was it said revolution is inevitable because man is bad, and useless for the same reason?" I puzzled for a fraction of a second. Voltaire? Montesquieu? One of the old French farts.

"If we had informed and active citizens we wouldn't need revolution," Beanie declared. "A real democracy where citizens actually monitored those who govern us."

"Informed citizens?" I laughed again. "Informed of what? and by whom? Information is a commodity sold to the highest bidder. Anyway, it's too late; your needle's stuck, Beanie. Politics has abdicated to the global marketplace. It only exists on screens these days or in the polls, which is the same thing. Go ahead, tell people to mock the circus — it's fun, but hopeless in terms of influencing political will." I shook my head. "Politicians are just a spectacle of corruption. And the elites of all parties will just keep doing what they've always done: consolidating their power and reproducing themselves."

Beanie diddled with his hat. His head jerked up suddenly. "I'm taking up your time," he said, dismayed.

"No you're not." I'd make him pay for it. "By the way, Beanie: how were you treated the other night after your arrest?"

"Okay," he said.

"They knock you around?"

"Not really." Then Beanie jumped back on his stump. It was his nature. "It's the Wild West up in the sky — there's virtually no regulation! There's no regulation of helicopters!"

"Yep."

"If you protest you can get into trouble with the police."

"Don't I know it."

"They get you one way or the other. D'you hear about—" Beanie stopped in his tracks. "You know what I'm talking about?"

I had rulers, pens, and pencils on my desk, a sharpener, a couple erasers. I lined them all up in front of me, then I pulled Clio's eraser off to one side. I'd rubbed it to a nub.

"Yeah, I know what you're talking about," I said. "I had a little run-in long ago, in another life. I lived at the beach then, down in Oceanside."

"Oceanside?"

"Rent was cheap."

"And?"

"I flashed one of those high-beam flashlights on a chopper one night. I got beaten up." I swallowed the puddle at the bottom of my coffee cup. It was cold, but it was wet and my mouth was dry. I could feel Beanie's eyes fixed on me. I looked away.

I looked far away.

It was early summer, early evening, much like today only hotter, more oppressive. Okay, I was in a foul temper, but no more than usual back in those days. I hated my job, hated my boss, hated my life on a cheap street in a military town. Most of all I hated the helicopter patrols that swung overhead on a routine basis, blitzing my barbecues.

"I'd complained before," I told Beanie. "I took it personal. Get those fucking things off my back! I told 'em when I called to complain for the twentieth time. They told me to move."

Before they hung up, they'd let me hear their snickers. Their oily snickers.

I stared at the desk, at the pens and pencils.

I'd gotten a couple of burgers out of the fridge that night and had taken them out to the barbecue. I'd built up a nice little fire, the coals were braising good, when I heard the telltale whop in the distance and the thunder closing in, till out of the blue a chopper loomed above the treetops and hovered right over my house. It stayed there, jack-hammer rotation, punching dust in my eardrums. They were trying to stir me up was all—have a little fun—and they got what they wanted all right. When the buns flew off the top of the grill, that did it. I stormed to the kitchen and got my flashlight. Take this and stick it up your ass! I bellowed to the machine and the buggers inside. I gave them the finger again and again, then I switched on the flashlight and shined the beam straight up at the pilot's eyes.

The chopper dipped. I stepped back, did a pirouette. The engine revved and pulled up right above me till I tore down the driveway and jumped on the hood of my car in order to keep a bead on them. The chopper pulled a fast fade behind a line of trees. The thwacking noise dropped to a drone. Then silence. The bark of a dog.

I'd stood there a couple of minutes, my anger alive inside. I went back to my backyard and was starting to wipe the twigs and dirt off my burger buns when I heard the screech of the cop cars. Next thing I knew I was flat on the ground, snotful of dirt. I wasn't conscious of the pain till later. I got kicked in the gut, kicked in the groin, couldn't count how many cops there were. When I tried to crawl away, I was grabbed and hog-tied.

"Fucking assholes!"

It was as if the sequence had been programmed from the start. I swept my hand furiously across the desk, sending the pens and pencils flying across the floor.

Beanie got up, placed his hat on his vacated seat, and went slowly around the room picking up my fallen pieces. He put them back in a neat pile on my desk, then came around the side and stood next to me. You could tell he wanted to put his hand on my shoulder but didn't know how.

"Did you press charges?" he asked.

I didn't answer at first.

"No. I couldn't stand the idea of spending all that time with lawyers. Life's too short. After that I buttoned up."

"You're lucky you weren't killed," Beanie said. "A guy in Pacific Palisades shot at a police helicopter a few years back. He committed suicide afterward, the local paper said. 'A troubled man.'"

After Beanie left, I got up, turned off the machines, put his file away and the pen and pencils. The easy part of closing shop. Wrestling with the outside gate was the other. I pushed up my sleeves.

I would oil the thing next week. Sure I would. And clean my shingle.

Everything was falling apart. Even the sidewalk seemed held together by chewing gum. A fresh piece glistened inches from my door. I picked up a piece of cardboard from the gutter and scraped up the wad.

I don't know why I walked toward the park. Maybe I was thinking Clio would be there and we'd bump into each other. Maybe it was the promise of Buddhist monks, the call to purity and longevity, the call of the lotus and all it represented.

The language of flowers, like all the others, watered with illusions.

Twenty

I wasn't alone. Streams of people were converging on the park, drawn by the sounds of live music that seemed to rise and swell over the lake before decanting in stray phrases over the surrounding neighborhood. I went with the flow and ended up on a trodden patch of grass at the center of a ring of food booths. The grounds were littered with Sa-tay sticks and soda cans; the smell of syrup laced the air.

She wasn't there.

I fought my way over to the lake. The lotus display was there, living up to its billing. Hundreds of flowers floated high over the north end of the shore, above the still waters and the raft of platter-sized leaves. Some Boy Scout had cleared out the grocery bags, leaving the focus on the pink-petaled blooms with the centers like yellow saltshakers. Hundreds of other plants, not yet in flower, raised their fat buds in prayer.

A Japanese company was crossing its fingers, too, hoping festival shutterbugs would use its brand of film. A blimp stationed overhead flagged the name; management wasn't taking chances.

When a ceremony of sorts broke out at my elbow, I merged back into the stream of people and was carried along this time over the footbridge and onto the park's island where I was dropped, like driftwood, in front of a tortured tree exhibit. Aldo would've loved it here, I thought. Clio, too, of course.

A man clasped my sleeve. "Bonsai should be pruned in round shape," he told me. "Round is the contour of harmony; round is the way of the universe." He invited me to sign up for a beginner's class of the Los Angeles Asian-American Bonsai Society. He said it would be good for me. "Become round!" he urged. "You all angles."

Everybody had a hustle. I should've handed out my business cards.

She wasn't here either.

I found one display of interest; it was sponsored by UCLA. Among the felt flags and sweatshirts and fliers for extension courses was a pile of lotus seeds—funny-looking things, like miniature footballs—plus a series of laminated information sheets. I learned a lot. Like how a lotus seed twelve centuries old was sprouted under the care of a university botanist, then dried to death in a hundred-degree oven so that the botanist could carbon date the value of what she'd killed. And how another seed from the bottom of the same Chinese lake had also germinated and even lived for some months as a plant in a pot before also becoming history, thanks to the same botanist's lack of gardening experience. The last seed in the magnificent accession had been given to one of the botanist's colleagues, a researcher specializing in enzymes that retard aging. He'd found what he was looking for in the lotus seed: money. He hoped one day to splice lotus longevity genes into commercial food crops.

In the meanwhile he had patented an idea for a lotus skin cream.

Intellectual property.

I swiped a bean. No one noticed. The crowd was turned on itself, intent on pleasure.

I threaded my way over to the entertainment area; maybe she'd be there. Spectators were scarce in front of the first of the stages; only a few stragglers cared to see *Hello, Dolly!* performed by the women of the Philippines Senior Citizens Center, and Clio wasn't among them. I watched the ladies kick for a while and when that got old, I meandered over to the other staged attraction: ten hipsters making music with various folk instruments including a selection of soup spoons. They'd attracted a big crowd. I scanned the audience. Lots of Shannas here.

And then, across the span, there she was. She didn't see me, but I could see her. I could see her all right. She had changed from her shapeless shift of the morning into a wisp of a sundress scooped in all the right places. You could see her head bobbing to the rhythm, see her long neck with the hint of giraffe as she leaned over and spoke into the ear of Mr. Ennui.

"Cotton candy?" A vendor thrust a cloud of pink fuzz in my face. I cursed and shoved it aside. The vendor cursed me back.

Their heads were still together. Ennui was nodding in

agreement. They left the grandstand area and slipped into the crowd.

Soup spoons tinkled, washboards clashed. The lead trianglist grabbed the microphone and broke into a vigorous acoustic transition to something I wasn't sticking around to appreciate. I was busy shouldering my way around the back of the audience, trying to keep Clio and her friend in my sights.

I lost them once—I played it too safe behind a flap at a food stand—but I spotted them again as they passed the Philippine chorus line and finally caught up with them at the footbridge to the island. They stayed there for a few minutes talking while I stood behind a nearby tree and ate bark. When they left the park I kept on their tail, I kept on them till they turned right onto Sunset and a half block up stopped at one of those retro cars and Clio got in the passenger's seat. I turned away then. I knew enough. I knew Clio was going for a ride.

There were two ways home from the festival: Heart Attack Ridge or the geriatric route. I took the easy grade. It meant circling the hill and walking three extra blocks, but I didn't have the spunk to fight gravity.

The streets were empty, empty of people and cars. I guess they were all at the festival.

I was wrong.

Up ahead, just past the last turnoff to the ridge, the cliffs fell sheer to the sidewalk. For two hundred yards there were no side streets, no structures, no nothing—just a sheer wall of sandstone, crumbly as Parmesan, its face pocked with crannies and holes.

The perfect spot for a drop.

A punk was pushing a fat envelope into one of those nooks. He looked up, saw me looking at him.

There were two ways home from the festival. Geriatric was one thing; dead meat was another. I hung a quick right up to Heart Attack Ridge. Twenty yards up the 38-degree slope I ducked behind a bush and peered back through the foliage. It was like I thought: the kid was too cool to work up a sweat. I stood there for a moment and panted. A flock of parrots lighted on a nearby branch. They were shy birds; it was rare to spot them so close. They must've taken me for a tree stump.

"Polly?" I asked as I stepped back onto the street, but the birds had forgotten their lessons.

I took it slow up the last of the slope, licking the side of my arm where the cotton candy had crystallized.

The truck was still there, in front of the clapboard house. Three days in a row now it hadn't budged. It was bad enough it was parked there nights and coughing soot in the mornings while its engine was being choked. The owner was really pulling our chain.

They were stopping at the Short Stop now, hoisting their first in a string of get-loose brews. He was searching his pocket for change to feed the juke, choosing something thick and juicy that would start to pulse as he moved back to the counter, as he brushed his meaty hand across the small of her back.

Mr. Ennui, I-Am-Me.

The small of her back.

There was a game on TV tonight, but I didn't have the stomach for it. It wasn't so much that the Dodgers were losing, it was their attempts to rebound I found so pathetic. At any event, I couldn't have watched. I had to deal with ants again. A squad had managed to crawl onto my arm where they'd picked up the scent of cotton candy.

With a warm, wet, dripping rag, I slowly dissolved and lifted the sugar, then dipped, rinsed, and wrung again. The cloth was homespun, rough against my skin. Drip, rinse. Wring again.

I was thinking purple—the purple prose of the Russian steppes. I couldn't stop myself.

Drip, rinse. Wring again.

He was steering with one hand like you do in those kinds of cars, switching from lane to lane in the thick Friday night traffic, advancing by way of voids. "Let's skip the club," he said.

"I don't get to dance much these days," she said, lowering her eyes. "He's not much of a dancer."

"We'll dance, baby, don't you worry. We'll dance." He reached over and ran his hand up her thigh. "The night is young."

A moment later he turned to her, eyes glimmering with reflected headlights: "Let's go to my place first. Don't say no. You've got my pecker in a state."

She laughed. He was so frank! Then she said: "I shouldn't of had that last beer."

"You shouldn't of been born with that body! Oh baby— come to me."

"Oh, I don't know."

"Fuck Joe."

Vroom. Vroom.

He swung into an alley littered with fabrics and broken bottles and jerked to a stop before a graffitied metal door. He took her hand. "Cop a feel," he said.

"Oh my."

With that he slid across the vinyl seat and muscled his tongue down her throat. The chrome door handle dug into her back as he parted and sundered again and again her wet mouth.

"I shouldn't of had that last beer," she repeated when she had a chance. She wiped her mouth.

"Fuck the rules, my little flowerpot. You're an artist."

"Oh, I . . . I don't know . . ."

He didn't want to hear. He pulled her through the dark hallway, up the stairs and into the sudden space of his studio lit by the moon and the stars through the floor-to-ceiling windows and, from within, by a series of halogen lights he'd installed to illuminate his towering rusted parts in pinpoints of brilliance.

But he didn't want to show her that — that was last season. He'd worked through his ennui and was now into vitality. He showed her his new work, threw her up against one of the latest in his series of massive, surgent, hammered bronze phalluses. "What do you think?" he asked, his words strangled by his thickened tongue.

"It's huge."

"We'll dance now," he agreed, grinding his pelvis into hers, using his art for purchase.

There would be no clink of bones as they coupled; for once Clio would be cushioned against layers of pumped tendon and tissue and molded brawn of this humping padded mechanic of a man tearing off his T-shirt, rubbing skin-to-skin against her bouncing bared breasts, Clio now held high above him with his hard Stallone sculpture-shoveling biceps, now spread back like a petal against his bronze burnished dong, now waiting wet at his altar as he slowly reaches down, lowers his zipper, pulls out his goods and drills her at last with his warm, fat, riveting cock.

A lone ant crawled confused up my arm, looking for the candy. It hadn't gotten the message. The candy was gone.

I squished it dead.

I was getting a lot of reading done at night. I'd trotted out my nail polish, too, and resumed work on my map of Simenon. There was a certain comfort in my return to routine, as though slipping into a favorite pair of socks that had been stored, lost, and resurrected.

I lowered the stylus on the *E Major Fugue,* sat back in my armchair, arranged the folds of my bathrobe. As the music kicked in I popped the top of my second beer. Certain of Bach's fugues were orgasmic, and this was one of them. Every voice had its own word, and it was pathos. Only Bach could keep it controlled.

I had to turn up the volume. A stray cat was howling in the garden. The season was long this year.

Then the phone started in again.

I'd had an answering machine once, but it'd gotten on my nerves. The voices had a way of haunting you if you didn't return their calls. Better not to answer at all. People gave up. Except the hardened cases, that is. The ones who had your number. Like this one. Bach was getting pummeled by the insistent ring. I steeled myself against the intrusion and at last—at last—the ring went away. If only that cat outside would disappear, too. But now there were two of them! two fucking felines! I jerked open the door and hurled my can of beer. Almost instantly I regretted it. The garden was looking bad enough as it was, and then it put me out of a brew.

I stood motionless on the stoop, tried to reabsorb my music lessons. After a long moment, I went back to the kitchen to get another beer and when I returned, Clio was in the living room.

She looked down at my feet.

"Come right in," I said finally. Slowly, with dignity, I retreated to the bedroom to take off my socks.

"The door was open," she said when I got back.

I didn't say anything.

"I was afraid maybe you were sick. I've been calling you nonstop the last three days. What's going on?" Her anger was building. "You could've answered. Don't you owe me that?"

"Can I get you something to drink? Beer? Orange juice?"

"*Have* you been sick?" she asked. Her voice lost its edge and gained in complexity. Socks = Sickbed, she was hoping. "I'll take an orange juice," she added when I didn't answer.

I was running low on oranges. I made a mental note to myself: Carlos still owed me . . . sixteen sacks.

When I returned from the kitchen Clio was peering at June Barry's calling card. She'd picked it up from the dish on the entry table. She looked up at me, surprised. "Are you going to call her?" she asked.

"Who?" I said, setting down her glass.

"June Barry. You've got June Barry's card here," she repeated.

"I don't know," I said. "Should I?" I added after a pause.

"Yes, I think you should. I think it would be good for you. It would open things up."

I nodded thoughtfully and then suggested she take off her jacket and stay awhile.

"I didn't come to stay," she said, taking off her jacket. "I left my black sweater here. I think it's in the hall closet." She found the sweater, set it down next to her orange juice.

"Started the résumé yet?" I asked.

"No, I haven't." She sat down on the edge of the armchair. I could feel her breath on my neck. After a moment she said, "Is this that Bach fugue?"

"Yeah."

The moments marched on through a range of tones and variations of material transformed in different keys.

And then the inevitable: the hand on my shoulder. "Joe . . ."

I stood up.

She got up, too, gathered her sweater.

Just as she was walking out, I called her back. I called her name—her silly advertising moniker—and swung her around and held her tight. She melted then with relief, but when I didn't let up and when I pulled her into the bedroom, she held back a second and said she shouldn't of come, and then she really did regret it because I started banging her, really banging her until the wall shook.

You hear, George?

Afterward she left in a hurry. She took her sweater and, along with it, her gardening books and records and earplugs and toilet kit.

Twenty-One

The wind had been howling all night long; as dawn broke it continued its havoc. I peered out from under the pillow. You could tell a Santa Ana just by reading the light. Sharp as daggers.

I had another hard-on—third morning in a row. I rolled over and worked it off to the beat of a branch that scratched the window with every gust.

I got up, drank my coffee black.

A neighbor's fence was toppled. Clio's garden was flattened, too, buried under blown newspapers and Styrofoam packing peanuts and more downed branches. Not that it looked any better under the debris. It was surprising how fast a garden could degenerate. A lone sprig of felicia survived the resprouted grass; now the wind was giving it a whipping. Aldo's lavender, under the bedroom window, was about the only thing still on its legs. Bones, that's what she'd called them.

I set out for work, head down, eyes slit against the swirling dust, dodging the palm fronds that dropped about me like missiles from heaven.

You could smell the damn truck a block away with this wind. It was true, the odor had gotten worse the last days so I guess I shouldn't have been surprised to see the cop cars pulled up or the ambulance and the stretcher and the lengths of yellow tape cracking in the wind. I pinched my nose as I approached. I didn't look at the body.

"Know anything about this, mister?" one of the officers asked, his words sucked out of him.

"No. Nothing," I said and I kept walking. It was none of my business.

Nonetheless, I stopped for a minute at Hair Today before I opened up next door. Teresa liked to be the first out the gate with gossip, and my news was hotter than a pistol.

She didn't want to hear it. The moment I walked in the door she jumped on me—with the strangest expression on her face.

She had news of her own.

"Mr. Will Brigham!" she announced. "You've got a visitor. Oh boy, do you have a visitor! I put her in your office."

"Put who?"

"Corazon Whosit's—your bride from Manila!"

"Corazon Casalong?" My eyes glazed.

"The taxi driver's in there, too. He says he's not budging till he gets paid his $45 and he says the clock's ticking."

"Forty-five bucks?" I said, my stomach starting to sink. Forty-five bucks was real.

"She took a taxi from the airport. Corazon Whosit's. She took a plane from Manila. You only have to pay from LAX."

I'd never seen Teresa so excited. This was the face of vindication, and it was glee. I peered around the edge of our adjoining door. There it was, all right: the pleated skirt.

"Teresa," I said, voice tight, "could you pay off the taxi driver? And stall the girl?" I fished in my pockets, found a couple twenties and a ten and thrust them at her. "Where's Willy?"

"He ran. He's in hiding."

"The hell he is," I said, already out the door to the back hall of the Jensen Recreation Center. I'd never been to Willy's apartment before. He'd never invited me, not that I would've gone. He lived on the top floor, underneath the neon bowler.

I took the stairs two at a time. I was puffing by the time I got to number 306.

"I'm not in!" Willy cried through the door I was pounding.

"Oh yes you are!" I hurled back. When I started to kick, he ceded.

Stacks of girlie magazines and videotapes. On the wall, pinups of the brides in various poses and positions. In a corner, the inflatable doll.

"Okay, Willy," I said, slow and tense. "Let's get this straight: you're taking care of this. This is none of my business."

"Bullshit. You're in this too," he said, holding onto a table.

"You go down there and apologize to that girl—make up something—and give her the money for a ticket back if she needs it. Pronto. And while you're at it, you can reimburse me for the fifty bucks I shelled out for the taxi."

"I can't do that—what about the girl? That's not right. She came all this way. Anyway, I don't have the money, not yet at least." He struggled. "Joe, let's be square here. We can't just dump her after what we did. Take her for a while. She's had a long trip, let her stay a bit."

"In my place?" I squealed.

"You played with her, too, you know."

You could hear the wind up here, hear the wind test the strength of the structure above our heads. I wondered when it would fall.

"You've got to keep me out of this," Willy went on. "You're going to add to her misery by making her stay with me? Listen Joe. Just take her for a little while. We owe her that."

I closed my eyes to clear my head, but the vision of the room was laminated on my lids, and the wind howled through the vacuum.

I turned around, steamed back down the stairs.

It wasn't the pinups that got me, it wasn't even the life-size doll. It was the glossy of me, framed—on a doily—dead center on the top of the bookshelf.

Willy called down after me over the railing, "Don't worry, Joe. We'll work something out."

At least she didn't call me Daddy.

"Will?" she said tentatively as I pulled back the gate to Joe's Word and opened the door as though nothing had happened, as though I didn't have a mail-order bride waiting for me in the client's chair.

We looked at each other across the floor.

"I . . . I wasn't sure this was right place, but the lady next door say it is." She was wearing the complete Pavlovian outfit. In her lap was a purse that looked like a lunch box. Her bags were at her feet. She set the purse on my desk and made a move toward me.

"One second," I said, sidestepping her approach. I locked the connecting door and closed the air vent. When I turned around, she was still there. "You must realize that this is a shock to me, Corazon," I said.

"I know. I know be better to ask first. But we so close in letters, I am thinking . . ." Her face screwed up. "Oh, Will— you not welcome me?" She came up to me.

"Of course, I do. It's just that . . ." I put my hand tentatively on her shoulder—something seemed called for. She was very small and very cute, cuter even than in her photograph. ". . . it's just that in person, I can be quite stiff. I thought I wrote you that, Corazon. I'm not much used to contact."

She smiled up at me and slipped her hand into mine.

The wind rattled the windowpane.

She was here on a two-week tourist visa. She told me if she'd had connections or money for graft, she could've stayed a whole lot longer.

I let her have my bed. I slept on cushions on the living room floor. I figured I'd give her a week.

The first day she told me about failed agrarian reforms, computer factories on Subic Bay, and Muslim insurgents in Mindanoa. Because I asked, she told me. But that wasn't what was on her mind; by later that night, she'd started brushing against my chest, and before the next day was out she was on my lap.

I'd come home late. I was seated barely two minutes before she'd sat down next to me and draped a richly woven fabric around my neck. It was impossibly long.

"Thank you, Corazon. How sweet."

"It go like this," she said, tucking and feeling me up with her fuschia fingernails. "You wear for ceremony," she chirped. "You like me to show you Philippine bird dance?"

"No. Not now," I added with an effort. "How was your bus ride?" I asked as she continued to stroke me and the scarf. I'd bought her a bus pass and explained how to use it. "Did you get to the beach?"

"I don't go. I want to be with you at beach," she giggled. "We go together?"

It was dusk and dark inside the room. I switched on the lamp and in the sudden bright light she loomed larger than ever, there was no avoiding her. I picked up and examined one of her hands, her puppy skin smooth and elastic. But that was a mistake, she took it for a go. She wrapped her arms around my neck and jumped on board, toppling a pile of books in the process.

Her weight was now cupped over my crotch and a fresh stretch of thigh exposed. She gave me another giggle.

"Corazon," I said, after a tricky minute. "Will you please do me a favor and wash off your perfume?"

She looked at me wide-eyed, but she left my lap and I was able to breathe again. I walked over to the front door. Corazon joined me a couple minutes later and together we watched the remains of Clio's garden in the growing gloom; our bodies, with the lamp behind us, cast shadows over the plot.

Corazon finally broke the silence. "What is happening to rose garden?" she asked in her high young voice.

"The rose garden was a figure of speech," I said, feeling suddenly very tired and very silly with this scarf around my neck. "That's what we writers do. That's our job. We try to be oblique."

"Will . . ."

"Joe," I said, too loud. There it was; it had to come out sooner or later. "The name is Joe."

She hesitated; there was a long pause. Then: "Don't you like roses?"

It was my turn to be stunned. I looked down at this lovely young girl, and I wanted to go to bed. Alone. On the living room floor. And that's what I announced, too, although it was only nine P.M. "Jet lag," I told her and she nodded and took out my bedding and plumped my pillow. She knew something was wrong, but she was thinking she would make it right.

And she did, the very next night.

I'd taken her to the Brite Spot for dinner and diversion—she was tickled to eat at a Route 66 coffee shop—but eventually the lights were turned off overhead and there was no escaping the route home.

As we left, Belinda gave me the thumbs-up sign.

Corazon started in before I'd even taken off my jacket. "Whoa!" I joked. I put on a Hank Williams record while she waited on the love seat—maybe he'd dry things out. I sat down and reached for a book.

But she couldn't live with the competition. "Will," she said, so sweet, "why you so shy? Don't you like me?"

"I told you my name was Joe. Joe," I repeated. I couldn't believe I was in this ludicrous set-up.

"You always be my Will," she said, snuggling close. "I am thinking, you know? . . . I have something more to give; not just scarf. Remember our letters, Will? Remember how I write about my favorite body part?" She moved closer still, she was rooting under my armpit. "I am thinking . . . maybe you want to see it?" She looked up at me. It was a look with a money-back guarantee. "What you want you can have, Will," she murmured.

"Cut the crap, Corazon," I said.

"What?"

"You know what I mean. Where'd you get the cash to come here? Don't tell me the money I sent multiplied like bread at the Sea of Gallilee. Where'd you get the money?"

"Secret!" she said, with an embarrassed giggle this time.

"And you can cut the giggles while you're at it, too. Don't act the innocent little schoolgirl with me. I know what you've got on under that skirt, and I'll bet you a million dollars it ain't made of cotton." She sat there staring at me. What the fuck. Maybe I was wrong. "This is no good, Corazon, no matter how you look at it," I said when I couldn't stand it anymore. "You don't know me. I'm no good; I'm not a good man."

She laid her hand gently on my thigh. "You good man, Will. I can tell. I know you write me about fancy office and fancy home and rose garden. You want to look good, many people do that. I see the letters you get here and the sign at the office with name of Joe. I don't know why you do this, but is no matter. What matter to me is not the name, but the man. And you a good man, Will, I can tell." She trailed a finger through my hair and when she ran out of material, she traced my lips. "I am young, but I know some things. I know that only angels live on top floor. And I don't want to live with angel."

She moved onto my lap then, onto my basement, and began to execute the man/woman thing.

The cherry lips, the sweet little nose, delicate at the bridge, broad and flat at the base where the nostrils now flared with excitement. The tight flesh of her thighs where my hand fell, fell of its own weight, to grope the deep of her pleats and finger the silken panties embroidered with lace . . .

I was no angel, no. I was only human. And when you've got a twenty-year-old with one hand on your balls, there's only one thing that's firm, and it's not your resolution.

Twenty-Two

The glee had gone out of Teresa's demeanor, replaced with a cold wariness. Although she wanted me and Willy to pay for our sins, I was her paycheck and Willy was mine. So she tried to steer clear of the Topic of Corazon.

"Has she gone yet?" she rumbled.

"Who's that? Who's here?" Mrs. E. wanted to know.

"A little special delivery packet," Teresa told her, and Mrs. E. nodded as though she understood. Teresa looked at me again. "Well?"

"She's going tomorrow night."

"Tomorrow? Friday night? In the middle of the tourist season? She got a reservation?"

"Cut me some slack, will ya?"

Teresa grunted and turned back to the counter where she'd been spooning up bowls of Gloria's latest, Fabulous Figs, and splashing its macerating juice on top. She held out a dish for me but I declined. The figs looked tired and shriveled and disturbingly like my balls.

Corazon and I had been at it like rabbits.

"Figs are supposed to be the real apples of the Garden of Eden, did you know that?" Mrs. E. threw out, glad to contribute to the conversation.

"Really," said Teresa. "That's surprising. It always seemed to me that biting into a fig was an act of faith."

I groaned.

"What's wrong, Joe? Indigestion?" Teresa pushed the fruit at me again as though it was a form of penance. "This is just what the doctor ordered."

"I'll have some more if it's all right with you—and could I have a bit more of the gin?" Mrs. E. said.

Gloria walked in with the new espresso machine. "Here comes our ticket to ride," she announced, setting the carton on the counter. "I had to park all the way over by the lake," she complained. "You'd think with all the money the Park Board raked in with that festival they could spend a little on that smelly lotus bed. It's full of muck and garbage. Hey, Slim! Heard about you and the bride. That's so cool! Way to go, Joe!" She gave me the thumbs-up sign.

"Bride?" Mrs. E. blinked.

"And what about Clio?" Teresa shot back at her daughter. "Clio, Clio."

I got up to go; I didn't have to take this.

"Where's Willy? He's usually around," Mrs. E. said. She was a real chatterbox this morning. "Is he sick?"

"I'll say," said Teresa.

"Has anyone seen Beanie?" Gloria asked. "I wanted to ask him more about that intestinal germ, but he wasn't in his usual place."

"He's probably in Hollywood," I told her. I knew where she could reach him at night, of course, but I wasn't about to send her there. If she pushed it, I could leave him a message. She didn't push it. She started talking about the line of desserts she wanted to sell at Hair Today. She and her mother were in negotiations.

I poured myself another cup of endangered drip and took it back to my desk.

Clio wasn't coming in till four, which gave me plenty of time to work badly and muddle. She'd sent me a postcard suggesting a time when we could go over Mrs. Evans' résumé. It'd come to that.

I looked through the pile in my in-box. I knew what should've been a priority. The letter from Natasha was three weeks old; she'd be wondering if I were coming to the rescue. Good neighbor Vlovnik, despite his advanced state of potato intoxication, had managed to knock me out cold and when I'd come around, I'd found him mounting my wife. I'd crawled naked onto his back but was no match for his brute force, and the last thing I remembered—before I'd lost consciousness the second time—was the sound of sleigh bells. Vlovnik had sacked Natasha and was sledding off with her down the road.

The problem wasn't with Natasha's plot. You'd have thought it'd been a snap to carry on Willy's work the way I'd been thinking lately with my dick. But it was a conflicted dick. The only time it knew what to do was when it was face-to-face with snatch; then it was hard and self-centered.

I thought of my framed phototograph on Willy's shelf. Had that really changed anything? Was I fooling myself?

I tossed Natasha back to the in-box. In the meanwhile there was that eulogy to write. It would put money in the bank. Good, clean money.

My client was the best friend of the deceased. I'd interviewed him much the way I interviewed job candidates. I'd tried to keep the tone professional, and for his part, he hadn't cried.

What were Mr. Springer's abilities and accomplishments? I'd asked. What made him unique? What do you think he'd have liked to do if he hadn't been a plumber? Take your time.

To these I'd added a few questions I figured might help, like: Any physical peculiarities? Spiritual tendencies? How, why, and in what context had he left this world?

As I typed into the computer, I imagined myself gazing down from the podium at the tearful crowd in black:

> I was trying to decide, you know, what to say today. I wanted to keep it brief, but I found it's not easy to wrap up your best friend's life. You can talk up his accomplishments, praise his character—but it seemed the more you define a man, the more he slips away.
>
> I finally realized that what Mickey meant to me could be wrapped up in one word: his whistle.
>
> Those who knew Mickey, knew his whistle came from the bottom of a very big and generous heart. It wasn't just a talent he had; it was a literal expression of himself. Whether it was "La Traviata" or "You Are My Sunshine," Mickey carried his whistle through all walks of life, from his meetings at Local 212 and golf at Griffith Park to his work at swank addresses in the hills, leaving smiles in every wake.

There was a time long ago—before marriage to his lovely wife Lydia had determined a different path—when Mickey dreamed of taking his musical gifts to center stage. But he told me once he'd never regretted his decision to settle down. He said he'd been rewarded many times over by their union, much more than the applause of a thousand could ever do for an ego.

That was Mickey. A man of great sensitivity, who gave of himself, shared with others, and cared for his family, friends, and work because he embraced responsibility and knew the joy that came of it. He was a man who loved life in all its facets, and expressed it with a whistle.

And now we're left with only the memory of Mickey's whistle as it fades down the long corridor. [PAUSE HERE.]

If you're listening to me up there, Mickey [LOOK SKY-WARD], will you do us a favor and give us one more tune from over the rainbow, just for old time's sake? For you were my sunshine—you were the sunshine for a lot of us—and now we find it's night.

I wondered whether my client should thank his audience at the end of the speech. I'd never been to a funeral before and didn't know the protocol.

Willy walked in while I was reviewing my pen collection.

"Long time no see," I said.

"I figured you and Corazon would want to be alone."

"Yeah, well."

"Okay, I got the money for the ticket." Willy gave me an envelope. "How's it going, anyway?" he ventured. "Have you told her yet? Is she . . . friendly?"

I looked back at him.

"What d'ya think of Alvarez last night? Top of the ninth? Did ya watch?" After another silence, he reached into his jacket, extracted three twenties from a roll and pushed them over the desk to me. "The two of you go out and have yourself a good time."

I pushed the money back.

He left, I lunched, and before you knew it, I was back at my desk again, working on another installment of Aldo's sitcom.

Sergeant Ramsey had gotten the latest photos I'd sent, but didn't feel he could offer any encouragement. "For instance," he'd written, "this photo you sent of the cash and the big bicep? Who's the owner of the big bicep? You represent that the bicep belongs to an employee of the illegal car repair business, but this is only a representation." In sum, he told me it looked like I had two choices: 1) Resubmit the material documented by experts and signed by a notary public. 2) Move.

He'd recommended the second alternative.

He had some gall to put it on paper.

I got on the phone to Aldo, who'd just had his tires slashed. I read him Sergeant Ramsey's letter and told him that, just from the top of my head, I saw seven alternatives: 1) Resubmit, in which case he could find himself another hired pen. 2) Move. 3) Kill the gang leader and go into hiding. 4) Take pictures of the gang bribing the cops, hire an expert to attest to the film processing, and then go into hiding. 5) Bribe the cops himself and run the risk of a bidding war. 6) Pay the gang to relocate, shelling out for the cost of the move and new advertising, plus loss of both short-term and long-term revenue. 7) Give up. Be Zen.

I recommended number 7, but Aldo howled in my ear, "I can't be Zen—I'm Sicilian!" There was a pause and his voice turned dreamy. "Maybe I coulda been Zen one day. I was working on it with my topiary." Then he exploded again. "How 'bout this for an option: trying to screw them in small claims court. Maybe then they'd get the message!" He told me otherwise he'd have to consider number 3.

I drummed my fingers on the desk. Then I tried a little whistle.

"What was that?" Aldo asked peevishly in my ear.

"Tell me, Aldo, have you seen Beanie lately? Is he still sleeping by the freeway?"

"No, I haven't, but he isn't there every night, least not that I noticed. They razed the camp yet?"

"I don't know. Okay, Aldo, I gotta go. I'll look into small claims court; I have no idea if it makes sense."

He thanked me in Italian.

Three o'clock. There was that assignment Riff sent over late yesterday by messenger. I had time to do that. I retrieved it from the wastebasket, flicked off the sort of dubious matter a wastebasket attracts, smoothed the crumpled paper against my desk.

There was nothing to it, Riff had written in the cover letter: just incorporating a few last-minute items into the Psychographics Profile I'd prepared two weeks ago. He needed it fast. "And could you come up with another joke? The one you sent earlier wasn't funny."

Riff was right about entering the data. It was the joke that was beyond me. I tried. For forty minutes I tried to be funny,

I even tried to be riot, but my funny bone was missing and so was my get-loose partner.

She'd be here any minute, I thought. While I waited I kneaded her eraser, which by now I'd reduced to a twist.

"Hi, Clio."

"Hi."

I got up. "I thought we might take a walk around the lake before we got going."

"No, let's get this over with." Her voice was all business.

"Have you finished your lotus series yet?"

"Just about, thank God," she said with a strangled laugh. She laid her portfolio on the desk and reached inside for her pencils. We had yet to look into each other's eyes. "I heard about the girl," she said, still poking.

"Who hasn't," I said carefully. Then: "I'm just putting her up, you know. She's leaving tomorrow night. I'm sleeping on the living room floor."

Clio winced, then she looked at me. I tried to keep my eyes steady. "What are you telling me this for?" she asked.

I couldn't stand to look at her like this, across the desk, across a gulf ten miles wide and epicenter deep. The void. I laughed to myself: she'd left me with a void. She'd probably get a kick out of that if she could ever find the distance.

I remember her saying once—sometime long ago when we were still lovers—that if there were no voids there'd be nowhere to move to. I remember thinking at the time that it was hogwash.

"Okay, let's get this over with then," I said gruffly, jerking

open the drawer to the file cabinet and extracting my por-
tion of Mrs. Evans.

She showed me her art first, the line drawings of the
seedling, the sapling, and the mature tree heavy with fruit.
She'd spent way too much time on them. They were terrific.
They were upscale.

The layout was an elegant counterpart to the art. Each
visual had its own page with a headline, a series of call outs,
plus a short copy block beneath. On the front page, which
read GRANDPA PLANTED THE SEED, Clio suggested I
write about the Glendale nursery, getting grounded in the lore
and love of plants, and so forth. Inside the single-fold, under
I HAD THE SAP, I was to refer to Mrs. Evan's college degree,
her bilingualism, her assumption of horticultural responsibil-
ities. YOU GET THE FRUIT was where I should put the benefit stated in nursery owner's terms. The call outs there, she
continued, could be on the order of Experience, Exposure,
Communication Skills, and so on. "In the copy block you
could talk about gardening wisdom and the forty-five years of
digging in dirt."

"What about the data and my personal statement? Where
does that go?"

Clio flipped the layout to the back page.

I frowned. A moment later I said, "I'd have to rewrite my
personal statement so it wouldn't be redundant."

"I . . . Do you think you actually need it? What if you
worked the material into the copy blocks instead — abbrevi-
ated, telegraphic — so the information would be more invit-
ing? So it would be read." She paused. "That way we keep the

back page for the data, which is necessary but dull." She paused again. "Of course I could adjust the layout."

"No, no. You've got a good point. I'll have to . . . It's a handsome piece, Clio. It's simple and personal, easy to read. Mrs. Evans should get a great response from this."

Clio nodded but didn't look happy. Perhaps if I cracked a joke?

We talked listlessly about typefaces and then we were through. I watched her pack her paraphernalia back in her portfolio.

"Thanks, Clio," I said.

The dentista drilled away on the other side of the wall. I felt paralyzed. Clio made it to the door.

"I'll let you know if I get another request for a creative," I managed.

"Bye," she said.

"Bye."

After she left I picked up her old eraser from my desk. There wasn't much left of it.

"Bye," I said and I tossed it in the wastebasket.

Then I took the new one she'd left behind and pulled open my top drawer and laid it in my wooden ruler box next to the erasers of mine.

Twenty-Three

I came home the next night to a rose garden.

"Surprise!" Corazon cried, jumping up from the steps where she'd been waiting, scouting my arrival. She didn't want to miss my stunned look of delight. I struggled to supply it. "I know you be happy!" she enthused. "Here, I show you." She took me by the hand and introduced me around. "This is 'Barbara Bush,' this is 'Queen Elizabeth' . . . I get all celebrities!"

She must've seen the question marks dancing over my head. "George help me," she said. "He's so nice. He takes me to nursery."

Did George give you the money, too? I thought. Or was that another secret. But of course it was possible George had fronted the cash. Corazon was friendly with anything that moved, and the wonder was that her warmth was returned. She'd even won over Suzette, who'd offered to show her around the neighborhood.

Corazon continued to bubble about her garden. "But you know?" she said. "That cat watch me whole time. Give me creeps."

"Don't worry about it," I said. "What did you do with the plants that were here?"

"I throw away, they all dead — except one still alive, but not really. I throw away, too. The flowers very small." She cast an adoring smile on her wads of rose bloom.

"The plant with blue flowers?"

"Yes. Flowers are blue, but very, very small." She looked up at me. "Joe, honey?"

She was calling me Joe now.

"Yeah?"

"I'm so tired from the dig, dinner not going to be ready in time. I like to take bath. You mind? We going to eat late."

As Corazon drew her water she sang a little Philippine song in her little schoolgirl voice. The atmosphere was rank with déjà vu, and it got even more hoary when the phone call came. I was in the kitchen squeezing orange juice. Corazon got to it first. "Who speaking please?" she was saying. She was standing there clad in a towel.

I took the receiver and she took the hint. I watched her pad back to the bathroom, hair swinging back and forth over her tush.

"Yeah," I said to the caller.

It was Pete. Of course. He seemed to have a hot line to the steam bath. He didn't beat around the bush. "Way to go, Joe!" he said. "Got yourself a little Pe-king Pussy?"

I played with the phone cord. I wondered if his wife knew he spoke like this. "She's the cleaning lady," I said.

"Ah. Have you been dirty?" Even his laugh leered.

"What can I do for you, Pete?"

He wanted to tell me about Jenny. I told him to go to hell.

Afterward I sat by the phone and doodled on the scratch pad. I'd joked about it but I'd cut close to the bone: Corazon was my cleaning lady. I felt responsible for what had happened—what I'd done—that was why she was still here. But it was getting even more complicated than that. She cleaned the apartment and did my wash and prepared my evening meal. I didn't have to lift a finger, except when I screwed her, and even then she did most of the work.

When she came out of the tub, all pink and rubbery and young, I told her to put on her best outfit because I was taking her out on the town.

The town would be Echo Park, but it was possible to splurge.

The smog had returned. I guess because of her age, Corazon hadn't been affected by it—even with all her activity—but as we walked down Sunset I noticed whoever was walking behind us was. I turned around finally to see who was wheezing.

It was Willy, trying to keep up with our pace.

"Wait here, will you Corazon?" I said. I dashed back and cornered my client.

"What the fuck," I said.

"It's a free country," he replied. "This is a public street." He was looking over my shoulder at Corazon.

"Then let's go public! Come on!" I gave him a little shove. "Let me introduce you to your bride. Corazon will be so pleased to finally meet her darling Willy—her dear Daddy. Or should I say her Granddaddy?" I pushed him again. You could see him shrink in pain, but I didn't care; I enjoyed it. "Corazon!" I called out.

He bolted.

"Who is that?" Corazon asked when she reached my side.

I was still boiling. "He's a local character I thought you might want to meet. He used to sell peanuts at the baseball stadium. He had to run."

"I like to go to baseball sometime."

She slipped her hand in mine. I let it drop.

Ed Hutch met us in the parking lot entrance like a priest at the chapel door. "Joe! How great to see you again! It's been too long. Welcome—welcome—to Les Frères Taix." He passed us on to the hostess with instructions to treat us right.

"What a nice man," Corazon said as we were led to a front-room booth. I preferred a back room, but Corazon said, "Oh, Joe." Her skirt rode high as she swung onto the seat.

I grabbed at a passing jacket and ordered a scotch on the rocks. "Make that a double, will you?" I called after the guy. I didn't have to drive; I just had to steer.

I was making headway on my drinkee and sucking on a cube when the jacket reappeared, this time with a bottle of wine. "Compliments of Mr. Hutch," he said. Two twists of his wrist and he was giving me the cork to sniff. Corazon didn't drink, but she was thrilled by Hutch's gesture.

The place also had linen tablecloths, upholstered banquettes, trout almandine, and frog legs. There were no roaming violinists, though, and the waitresses were the seasoned types.

"What'll it be, hon?" one of them asked Corazon, hand on hip. Corazon ordered the Friday special, bouillabaisse; I took the braised short ribs. I swear, as the waitress left, she whispered to me, "Way to go, Joe!" Maybe it was the scotch talking.

I wondered what the wine would say.

I hit the bottle.

"This is heaven. I'm in heaven," sighed Corazon when the tureen of soup arrived. She loved the pâté, too. She was a sweet girl.

She laid down her fork suddenly and reached across the table. "Joe, honey? Remember the ride in the balloon you write me about? 'As high as eye can see?' Well, I just want you to know you don't have to take me on balloon ride. I know you don't have many dollar, and besides, make me seasick." She rubbed my hand.

"I guess we could go to the beach," I finally said.

"Oh Joe! Could we? Tomorrow? Oh Joe!" Her eyes were all over me. Under the table she worked her foot.

Her delight carried her all the way to the main course. She did all the talking; she didn't seem to notice the dark. If she didn't want to live with an angel, she didn't want to hear about the flip side, either. She still hadn't quizzed me, for example, on my name change and its connection to my work.

I poured myself more of the pricey wine that put me in Hutch's pocket.

"Look! Cary Grant!" Corazon giggled, pointing to my plate when the main course arrived. My ribs were garnished with a tomato carved like a rosebud. Corazon had to explain that the actor had a rose named after him, too.

When the dessert came around, so did Hutch. I lifted my

glass in thanks and introduced him to Corazon, who told him she was from the Philippines.

"Are you one of our residents? or just visiting?" Hutch wanted to know, and know more.

Corazon didn't reply. She glanced at me then smiled down at her lap. Then she picked up her fork again and resumed her attack on the chocolate chip cheesecake.

"Say Ed — do you know if that homeless camp has been razed yet? The one on Lucas Street the developer bought?"

"No, not yet. But don't worry, I've had a talk with my contact downtown. It doesn't look like their plans will affect us in any manner. Hey there, Vince! How's it goin'?" He waved at someone in the next booth and moved on.

I don't remember much how we got home. I remember, though, as we were getting down to business in the bedroom, I sensed something odd. I don't know if it was the sound or the scent. I think it was the smell of lavender, though, coming through the open window. Crushed lavender.

I stumbled into my pants and ripped out the door fueled with rage and swill. I caught up with Willy out on the street, out of earshot of Corazon and the court — not that it mattered, because when I spoke it was in a voice so tense and tight it had collapsed into itself. "Fuck you, Willy!" I said. "Fuck you and your money! I don't ever want to see you again. We're through — understand? Over!" Willy just stood there, mouth agape. He made me madder than ever. I kicked at his legs and missed. He moved a few feet away and stood his ground. "Get the fuck outta here!" I was shouting now. "Out! Out!" I kicked again and missed again and then it was in my blood. I chased him halfway down the block, only drunkenly aware of the helicopter the next street over. When a car screeched past the intersection, though, I came to my senses.

I looked at Willy, wheezing in a pool of lamplight.

I turned back to the court.

"But she's mine, too!" Willy sputtered after me. They were the first words he'd spoken. "She's mine, too—I paid for her!"

When I crawled back in bed, Corazon asked sleepily, "What was that?"

I told her it was just some animal.

Twenty-Four

I went off to work Monday morning earlier than usual. I wanted to take a swing or two around the lake. I was looking for peace, though it didn't look good.

The smog that had been hanging over L.A. the last few days was now mixed with morning fog. I had to take it slow. A fish, dark and dull, flopped its tail on the surface of the lake. What did it have to jump for? I stopped and watched the ripples until they disappeared.

Once around the rosy would be plenty enough, I thought, as I neared the lotus bed.

I saw her from a distance at first, hunched over her drawing board. She looked different somehow; it wasn't till I got up close that I saw she was wearing noseplugs. And I could see why.

She looked up, startled, from her concentration. "Is it always this smelly this time of year?" she asked as she took off the clamps. She laughed a little.

I laughed, too, and did about as good a job. "It's pretty bad, all right. They need to clean up this place."

"The transcendent lotus, rising from the muck . . ." she joked.

If she'd heard that Corazon was still in town, she wasn't saying anything. It was in the air, though, suspended with the fog and smog. The rubber pads of the noseplugs left pink spots on her flesh; they disappeared at about the same rate as the ripples on the lake.

I knelt down beside her, squinted at her subject and then back at her drawing board. There it was again, her gift for flowers. You wanted to touch her lotus petals and crush them in your fist.

These were the sort of thoughts I'd been fighting as I'd walked around the lake.

She tried to make small talk. "It's not easy to draw from nature, between the wind and the bugs," she told me. "Some flowers turn toward the light, too, and that throws your voids off kilter."

You could barely see the far side of the lake. The palm trees were shafts of dark against the mottled light.

"You still doing dogs?"

"I just got a commission to draw my first flower," she said. "One of June Barry's friends asked me to do a plant in her garden."

We were in deep muck. She couldn't be excited about that; I couldn't be happy for her, either. "That's terrific," I said. "Congratulations."

A flock of pigeons flapped noisily into the air and circled over our heads. My knees were getting tired; I wasn't as young as I used to be. "Well," I said, "I guess I'll be off, too.

I can't stand the smell any longer. Better put those plugs back on."

"I'll be finished tomorrow, thank God, 'cause it keeps getting worse. I'm afraid I'm always going to have these associa . . ."

"It's been getting worse?"

"Oh yeah."

I don't know why I hadn't made the connection. I guess it was a matter of expectations. I'd assumed the stink was grounded in rotten garbage or decaying roots in oxygen-deprived mud—something like that—but now, suddenly, my sense of smell turned acute. I knew what I was smelling was something I'd smelled before.

"What's wrong?" Clio saw the shadow that crossed my face.

I paced back and forth along the bank until I found the spot where the stench was most intense. Then I looked around for a long stick or fallen branch.

"What's going on?" Clio was at my shoulder as I started to fish.

It wasn't like I hadn't steeled myself. But it could've been a dog or a cat—why not? Instead, not five feet from the shore, hidden by the thick hedge of lotus foliage, my stick struck a badly decomposed hand raised slightly above the waterline as if signaling the presence of the decayed body beneath.

Half-submerged next to it: a small felt beanie with a dollar bill weathervane.

Clio made a sound behind me I hoped I'd never hear

again. I dropped the tree branch and took her in my arms. She was shaking badly and wouldn't stop. In a move that was so familiar, I held her tighter still. It was all as I remembered — the scent of her hair, the smooth of her neck. For an instant we were again two sides of the same ribbon. Then Clio stiffened and her self-consiousness snapped back into place. I stepped back, too, keeping a hold on her arm to steady her, and told her to stay put while I called the police.

I ran to the office, called 911, then raced back to the park with the flask of scotch I kept in my bottom desk drawer. I made Clio take a couple big hits and then I knocked one back myself. She waited propped under a tree. I stood out on the street and flagged down the black and white.

There wasn't much to it. They took our names and phone numbers and then they dragged what was left of Beanie out of the water and into a body bag. One of those high beams fell out of his jacket pocket. Probably what kept him weighed down in the water once his soul escaped.

Clio didn't watch. She went home.

It was going to be hard for her to complete the lotus series.

Twenty-Five

I made a pot of java at home and poured it into a thermos. That way I wouldn't have to go to Hair Today for my coffee breaks.

Beanie's murder had upset our circle, and the police reaction to it even more. We'd been told Beanie had died from a head injury, bludgeoned by a flashlight recovered at the scene. Since no money had been found on the body, their conclusion was formal. The killer: another transient. The motive: robbery. There were no plans to investigate.

Teresa had been galled, then galvanized by the official response. I think she was mad over what had been going on at Joe's Word and needed to ventilate. At any rate, first thing she did was put up a sign in her window that read BEANIE'S BIRTHDAY PARTY HEADQUARTERS. Inside, she'd started organizing, setting up a memorial fund for Beanie and trying to get the media on the case. She was doing all right on the memorial fund front. One of the first to chip in was the Echo Park fisherman; others trickled in off the street and gave what they could. Word about Beanie's death and the new HQ was passed the old-fashioned way, exchanged at street corners and over backyard fences, because on Teresa's other front — the media — involvement had been zip. "Naturally!" Teresa had griped, slamming down the phone one more time in disgust. "They're the vested interests Beanie was trying to break up."

The only newspaper to run anything at all was the *Echo*. It ran Beanie as an anonymous statistic in the weekly "Crime Blotter."

Gloria, too, had taken up the cause. She was trying to generate interest by logging onto the Internet. She believed Beanie may have been murdered because he had the goods on *E. coli*. Okay, it was unlikely — Beanie's speeches were two-bit, why should anyone care? — but in this day and age, you could never be sure . . .

In fact, apart from Pete and Ed Hutch, who agreed with the police, everyone had his or her pet conspiracy theory they thought warranted a closer look.

Mrs. E. felt there might be a connection between Beanie's death and the satellite/helicopter surveillance industry. She hated to think of anyone but God looking down on us. She'd stopped wearing her "Serenity" collar and had started asking questions. She looked like a stripped-down angel.

Clio's suspicion came as no surprise: Bt might be behind it, *Bacillus thurengiensis*, the soil bacteria that was being genetically engineered into food and cotton crops.

Aldo came by the headquarters, too, to tell us he had the scoop: Beanie's dormitory at the freeway sound wall had been discovered by the illegal car repair/stolen car ring, and to ensure his silence, Beanie had been offed.

Willy wasn't saying anything because he was staying out of the picture.

As for Teresa, she wasn't placing her bets, either—not till she'd had an answer from me about what the hell Beanie had been doing as my client. I'd told her it had nothing to do with his death and that if word got out I was revealing my clients' personal matters to the police, she could kiss good-bye to Joe's Word, and to her paycheck, too. Yet that didn't seem to satisfy her. At least that was my guess when I passed Hair Today, cradling my thermos, and Teresa ran out and collared me.

"I need to talk to you," she said, frowning.

Over her shoulder, taped next to the Birthday Party sign was the long-heralded poster of Clio. THE CYBORG IS HERE! it read. NEW AND EXCLUSIVE AT HAIR TODAY!

"What's wrong with 'The Seberg'?" I asked, pointing to the window.

Teresa did a one-eighty. "Isn't that fabulous?" she said. "It was Clio's idea. The funny thing is that she really *does* look like a Cyborg. I got it up just in time. I've been getting great exposure with all the people coming in." Then the shutter came down again. "Joe. We gotta talk." She was trying to look me in the eye, but I couldn't keep mine off Clio.

"Go ahead, talk," I said. "I'm not stopping you."

"I can't now, I've got a customer. How about this afternoon?"

I looked inside. Sure enough, waiting in the swivel chair sipping an espresso, was a Shanna sheared halfway into a Cyborg. "I'm not staying that long," I muttered. "Better make it soon."

She rolled her eyes, then went back to work. I opened the gates to Joe's Word.

A fine layer of dust had settled on my desk. I hadn't been coming in much. In fact, I hadn't been doing much of anything lately, and what I was doing, I wasn't doing well. I'd been sleeping badly, for one thing, waking up two or three times a night from dreams full of lotus blooms and bloated bodies and flashlights. The sleeping pills I'd finally taken had only left me with more jitters. I wasn't much fun to be with, but it didn't seem to bother Corazon any. She remained relentlessly cheerful.

I'd given her some cash this morning to get a manicure, steering her to Teresa's competitor and feeling bad about it.

"She no good the lady next to you?" Corazon had asked as I'd started off to work.

"She doesn't do manicures," I'd replied. Corazon had looked at me funny, so I'd promised to take her and her hot new nails out for a beer tonight. She'd practically skipped back inside.

When I finished dusting my desk and electronics, I sorted through the mail. I leafed through a bride magazine before throwing it in the garbage. It left me cold. For that matter, so did the whole business.

Mrs. Evans had written a note thanking me and my art director for the wonderful job we'd done. If we ever got to Pasadena, she'd said, she hoped we'd stop by Burkhard's nursery and look her up. She especially wanted to invite my art director to come visit her own garden and take home some unusual plants.

I poured myself some storage coffee into the thermos cup. It wasn't bad, but it needed cream and I wasn't about to get it.

Not long after, Teresa rapped on the connecting door. I waved her in. She sat on the edge of the client chair and squared her shoulders forward. She looked like a linebacker.

"Let's have it," I said.

"A good-looking blonde was in my place asking for you."

"That's not what you're here about."

"Beautiful clothes. Beautiful hair. Unstyled," she couldn't resist adding. "She contributed to Beanie's memorial; she bought a jar of Gloria's jam, too. I told her I'd tell you she'd been by, but I forgot her name."

"I know who she is. Thanks."

"She came to my place because your place was closed." She glared at me. "Again."

I shrugged. What was I going to say? She had her facts right.

"We're behind on your billing, you know," she continued to egg, "and I need to go over your books."

"That's not what you're here about," I said. "C'mon. Out with it."

Teresa shifted in her seat an inch and straightened her back. "It's about Beanie," she said at last. "You could be hiding something, for all I know — information that could lead to the murderer." She paused, then blurted: "If I don't do anything, I could be an accessory."

"You've been watching too much TV."

"I have to, to keep up with the hairstyles. Joe. I'm serious. People have a right to know what he was doing with you."

I flattened my hand on the desk for emphasis. "Beanie had his mail sent here is all. Okay? All right?"

"Why didn't he use a post office box?"

"Why didn't he wear a tu-tu when he got on his soap box? Listen, Teresa, I'm telling you now: he just picked up his mail here. That's all."

I'd called downtown the day after Beanie's body was found. There'd been no funny business and no activity on his account other than his usual check. Beanie had wanted anonymity, and as far as I was concerned, he was going to get it. If the New York suits wanted to publicize his philanthropy, that was their problem.

Teresa played with the fringe on her shawl. I don't think she believed me. Then she changed the barbs in her arrows. "Tell me—is it true that Corazon's still here?"

I didn't give her the pleasure of a response.

"Willy said she was still here yesterday," she went on.

"So Willy has finally surfaced, has he? As an informer?"

"When was it exactly that Corazon came? Around the seventeenth, wasn't it?" Teresa held up her hands and started to count conspicuously on her fingertips. "Seventeenth, eighteenth, nineteenth, twentieth . . ."

I shoved back my chair too fast and it made a rent in the rug. I looked down at the floor, then back at Teresa.

She gave a little cluck and got up to go. The door banged shut behind her.

Twenty-Six

The Dodgers were continuing in their usual August slump. In the closing days of the season maybe they'd be topic number one, but for now they were dismissed by the patrons of the Short Stop. We were here to shoot pool, play darts, get stinko.

Except Corazon, who didn't know how to do any of that. She liked to play the juke, though, so I supplied her with dollar bills and she made runs while I downed my mugs of second-rate beer. I hadn't been to the Short Stop for a while. My favorite brand was no longer on tap, and that wasn't the only thing that'd changed. The decor, which used to be kitsch, was now stark and without character. Worse: fluorescent lights lit every corner of the room and washed out its at-mos-phere. Couldn't they let a guy drink in the dark?

Corazon returned from another session in the front room; "I Did It My Way" began to play. She swung her legs and sang along and eyed the cops in shorts.

That was when Clio walked in, clutching a cue stick.

What was she doing here? This was *my* bar. She'd been

drinking, that was for sure, and seemed to be using her cue as much for support as for swagger. She went directly to the pool table, laid a quarter under the edge, then scanned the room for a partner.

There was a bad moment when she saw us. She tried to hide it, but the fluorescent lights made no allowance for grace.

She came over to our table.

"Hi Clio," I said. "How you doing?"

"Not sleeping."

"That makes two of us. Clio, this is Corazon. Corazon, Clio."

"You a friend of Joe? I'm so glad! I like to have girlfriend here."

Clio stared at Corazon, then at me. Her voice cracked when she spoke. "It's *Bacillus thurengiensis*. I know it sounds crazy, but you should see what I'm reading about its connection to anthrax."

"You sit down, no?" Corazon smiled up at Clio and patted a seat. "Want some beer?"

"I've been going to the library every day to do research. Modified Bt can get into the wild population. It could . . ."

Corazon watched Clio with admiration. She threw me a smile to show me how much she liked my friend.

I interrupted. "You're not taking this seriously, are you?"

It was a second before Clio replied. "Maybe that's the problem. Nobody but Beanie was taking things seriously. It's already been proven *E. coli* can escape, so why not Bt? You know how? Lab coats in research facilities get splashed with bacteria, and when they're washed they go through the pre-wash cycle first—in *lukewarm* water, the perfect conditions for bacteria to reproduce!" She was babbling, but her voice held. "Then the prewash water is drained into the *sewer*, where the modified bacteria can mingle with all the other bugs that live there! It's beyond belief!"

Clio seemed to have a better grip on her research than she did on her tongue. It was touching the way she slurred *Bacillus thurengiensis*.

"There's a bunch more articles in professional journals, but the library doesn't subscribe to them. I think Beanie got to them. It may take time, but I'm going to get to them, too."

I finished my beer, which—I was more than ever aware—would soon drain into the sewer of close encounters. "I wouldn't bother," I said at last.

"No, of course you wouldn't."

Corazon patted the chair again. "Come sit down."

"Beanie's death has nothing to do with Bt or *E. coli* or Aldo's stolen car ring or any of that," I said.

"How would you know? Mr. Bump on a Log."

"Mr. Bump on a Log with eyes . . ."

Clio slid into a chair.

I lowered my voice. "The cops did it," I said without inflection. "I have my reasons, but I don't have any proof." I worked on the frost that covered my beer mug. Clio's eyes were riveted on me. I pushed the mug away, wiped my hands on my pants. "Plus you know the flashlight the police said was used to kill Beanie? It wasn't just any old flashlight. It was an expensive model, one of those high-beam types.

Would a transient—one so desperate for money that he's robbing another transient—really throw away such valuable merchandise?"

"How come you haven't reported this?"

"Even if the police looked into it, they'd whitewash anything that pointed to themselves. And the media would go along. It's not anything the authorities would want publicized."

Clio's face scrunched up. "But it's *got* to be investigated. You never know! How can you just shrug and look the other way?"

I shrugged and her face contorted more.

Corazon had stopped smiling. "Joe honey," she said, touching my hand. "Maybe we go home now."

Clio barely registered Corazon's intimacy. "You don't stand for anything, do you, Joe." she said, suddenly very cold. "You're totally spineless. You're just a totally spineless . . ."

I waited.

She shot a look at Corazon, then back at me. "You know who you are, but maybe you're suppressing it because it's so hard to stomach, so I'll tell you what. I'll give you a hint." She was spreading it on thick. "It has to do with Willy and services provided, and it begins with 'P.' "

I pretended to puzzle. "Public writer?" I asked.

For a tortured moment she was silent. Then she got up, whirled around and marched off.

Twenty-Seven

The next afternoon the cops showed up at my door. "LAPD," they said, as if I couldn't guess.

"What can I do for you?" I asked politely, ushering the two of them in. They didn't answer. They looked slowly and deliberately around the room.

"You live here alone?" the bigger of the beanstalks asked.

"Yes," I said. "What's this all about?"

"It's come to our attention that the Echo Park gadfly known as Beanie was one of your clients at . . ." he looked into a notebook, ". . . a business called Joe's Word." He looked up again. "You're a public writer?"

"That's right."

"What the heck is that?"

"I write for hire. I take anything on."

"You look familiar." His jaw jutted forward. "Ever go to the Short Stop?"

"Yeah."

"You should write about us cops, you know? We can tell you some stories."

I totally agreed with him.

"So what did you do for this Beanie character?" The investigation resumed. "Write his speeches?"

"I collected his mail and stored his checkbook for security. He had a local account. I've already called his bank. There was no activity either before or after his death. I'll give you the account number and you can check for yourself."

"You were the one who found his body, according to the report."

"That's right. Myself and a friend. It was a coincidence."

"Can I see your driver's license, please?" the big one said. He looked at it at length. "How come your number's so low?"

"It's the number I was given."

He grunted then passed the plastic to Junior, who took it out to the squad car. A moment later Junior returned and pulled the big guy into a tête-à-tête.

My hands started to sweat.

When the huddle broke up, the big guy declared, in a changed voice, "You've got a record."

"The embezzlement? That was a onetime fling," I joked. "I'm your basic model citizen."

"Obstructing police officers, endangering aerial support unit operations, resisting arrest: you call that being a model citizen?"

"But I was never charged! That's in your computer?"

Corazon couldn't have picked a worse moment to walk in, bag of groceries in hand. She looked at the officers, then at me, then back at them again. I could feel the hair on my head rise.

The cops perked up instantly. "Papers, please," they told her.

They gave her three minutes to pack. Junior watched from the doorjamb to see she didn't escape before she got to the INS.

"I going to love you, Joe," Corazon said, grabbing her skirt from the closet. "I going to marry for money, but I going to love you, too."

"You're a sweet woman, Corazon. I'm sorry. I'm sorry for everything."

"Not your fault. I know from beginning it maybe not work," she said. "Had to try something—had to, for my girls."

"Your girls?

"Speed it up," Junior said.

"Have two daughters in Manila. Be so good to see them!"

I followed her to the bathroom where she got her toilet kit. "You're kidding! Who's taking care of them?"

"Mom. I am missing her so much, too."

I drew a sharp breath.

"I could be going to Tokyo and be a maid, but I go for love. Am I wrong?"

Who was I to say?

Corazon tried to stop and smell the roses as she was being led away, but the cops wouldn't have it. She called to me over her shoulder. "You write a book about me one day, okay?"

"Okay," I said, trailing behind.

I watched the police car roll off. I'd never taken her to a baseball game.

Afterward I sat down on the stoop and let my pulse drop.

They'd seized on Corazon as a diversion. They hadn't intended to investigate me—or anyone else for that matter. They hadn't even taken down Beanie's real name and account number. They'd made the required house call. End of subject. Finished.

I got up, locked my door and, one foot after the other, started to walk.

It'd been a fierce August and today was on par. Heat shimmied above the asphalt, glanced off steel and concrete. You had to go slow and wade through it. The lady halfway down the hill said hi, like she always did, just as her dog barked and lunged till she said shush. Everything was as it always was—same time, same station—except for the sooty truck, which had moved on about the same time as its owner. In a way, you could say the neighborhood had improved.

In fact—now that I looked about me—it did seem some sort of beautification project was afoot. Sunset Boulevard had been planted with saplings; the Salvadorean was roasting corn in the feeble shade they gave. When had that happened? Where had I been? Even the pigeons seemed to be in on the effort, scratching the dirt, depositing droppings.

On the roof of Jensen's, workers were repairing the neon sign.

I passed Hair Today. It was full of activists, too. There were a couple new faces I hadn't seen before, one of them a Latina painting a banner spread on the floor. Teresa was hovering over her, giving directions. I noticed Willy was there.

Joe's Word. Cardboard clocks.

I didn't stop. I was just walking.

At the corner by the lake, I saw a flier for Clio blown into a blocked sewer drain. I saw her at the grocery store, too, when I stopped to pick up a pack of hamburger buns. I nearly said hi. Turned out to be a Cyborg clone.

Back home I made up a mess of fresh orange juice and sat down with a glass next to the phone. It was beyond hot, and beyond calm—the dead calm of the equator. I drank my orange juice and watched dust percolate through a rebel shaft of sunlight. I got up, drew the curtain tight.

Then I sat down again and made the phone call.

". . . You have reached the information desk of the Los Angeles County District Attorney. If you would like to hear this message in English, please press the pound sign now . . ."

". . . You have reached the information desk of the Los Angeles County District Attorney. If your call is regarding child support, call 728-1000 . . ."

A dozen options later I got the number of the investigations unit. I called. No one answered.

I looked at my watch. 5:06.

Hot damn.

I got myself a beer, put on a loud record and kicked off my shoes. I was only too happy to put off the unpleasantness until tomorrow.

Twenty-Eight

I poured myself another cup of coffee. It smelled like dirty socks. I sniffed the empty thermos and it was even worse. I made a note to myself to buy one of those cleaning gizmos.

Pretty soon now I'd make the phone call, but not yet. I had to gear up for it.

It'd been a long time since I'd done my own books; I remembered why I'd given Teresa the job. In fact, I'd have been happy if the numbers were merely boring, but I was finding the bottom line as bitter as the coffee—and I didn't see how things were going to improve. Conventional résumés were going the way of the dodo, plus I'd ditched my biggest client and now I'd lost Beanie, too. Riff, who'd had the look of a long-term cash cow, couldn't be expected to last much longer, either—not as long as I couldn't party on paper, and that wasn't in the cards.

On the bright side of the balance sheet, I could always write funeral speeches and tread water with Aldo.

I was in a hole, but I'd been there before.

I upped the speed on my desk fan, and the sweat left my forehead.

The second time I heard the knock I recognized it for what it was. I'd thought at first it was mice scratching—not that I'd ever had a rodent problem, but now anything seemed possible.

It was Teresa.

"I made up a pot of fresh coffee," she said, in a voice that was all artifice. "Drip. A whole pot. There's just me to drink it. Seems like kind of a waste."

She left the door open, and after a couple minutes of mulling, I followed her in, poured myself a cup and sat down in my old seat against the wall, under the banner that read THE PARTY'S NOT OVER. Reversed in the mirror it seemed more compelling: REVO TON S'YTRAP EHT. Teresa kept her back turned to me, busying herself with combs and solutions. The room was silent save for the slosh of the washing machine and the far cries of an ice-cream vendor. Above us, the piñata rocked from the wind of Teresa's powerful fan.

I picked up a hairdo magazine, but I'd barely begun to leaf through it when I heard a flutter over in my place. Teresa heard it, too. "Customer," she said, turning around. I glanced around the door and did a double take.

There, laying a piece of paper on my desk, was Beanie. Teresa was right behind me. She saw him, too.

I'd been through a lot lately. I'd been drinking too much. I'd been taking sleeping pills. I'd been mainlining coffee to get me through the day and rubbing young flesh to get through the nights. I'd seen cops and I'd seen corpses. But this went beyond the bend.

Teresa was the first to speak. "How in the hell am I ever going to refund your memorial money?" she said.

Beanie tripped into Hair Today. It was strange to see him out of uniform. He was wearing a cap, baggy pants, and an old promotional T-shirt and could've passed unnoticed in Echo Park if no one looked too close. One thing, though, was unchanged: the pale of his face. He may have been back among us, but he still looked like a man submerged.

"Okay, what's the story."

"I was leaving you a note."

"Go on."

"I figured I'd be more effective dead. And I was right," he added, though his tone was not triumphant.

"What about the body in the lake?"

"I didn't plan it—honest I didn't! I just stumbled on it. Literally. I stumbled on a dead body late one night in the park and I just ran with it—the opportunity, I mean. The man was dead anyway; I tried not to think about that part of it. I just put my coat on him and tipped him into the water."

"And put a high-beam in his pocket . . ."

Beanie looked at me, startled; his eyes darted quickly away. "I didn't like what I did—and afterward I regretted it—but people were apathetic, they weren't paying attention to the issues. They responded to me like some kind of personality. They romanticized me."

"That's just gruesome," Teresa exclaimed. "You're really sick, you know that? To think of all the time I've spent promoting you and your pathetic little party!" She swept across the room and ripped down the party banner. I wasn't happy either. No one likes to be used.

"But I was right, wasn't I," Beanie continued to defend himself.

Teresa gave the fallen banner a kick.

"You should've died young like Che Guevara; you would've had better press," I said dryly. "So what do you plan to do now—the first day of the rest of your afterlife?"

"It's in the note I left on your desk. I'm moving on, somewhere where people need to wake up. I've decided on Dallas."

"After you've gone to the police."

"It's all in the note."

"Good riddance!" Teresa said.

Beanie shook hands with me. Teresa kept hers behind her back. But just as Beanie was going out the door, Teresa called out to him. "Wait! Hold on!" She ran behind the partition and returned two seconds later. "Here's something for the folks at Dallas. I won't be needing it." She held out a big bag of confetti to Beanie, and as he reached to take it, she dumped it instead over his head. The blast from the fan sent the works in a flurry.

Beanie thanked Teresa politely and with great dignity walked out of our lives. That's how we remembered him later—a zombie who reappeared and disappeared again in a freak snowstorm.

I helped Teresa clean up the mess and then I left for home. In theory I could've worked a couple more hours, but I had a need to disconnect. This was just another patch I had to go through, I told myself, as I sunk into my armchair and caught the rest of the ballgame.

During the seventh-inning stretch I countered an ant attack, and while I was at it, I cleaned up around the court, sweeping the dirt and dust from the sidewalk into the garden plot. Who needed a trash bin.

Corazon's roses hadn't been watered since she'd left and hadn't survived the dog days. They were just sticks and parchment, from dust to dust and blah blah blah—just like Number 4's cat, which had been found sprawled under the avocado tree about a week ago. Number 4 had put its ashes in an urn and placed it on his TV set. Yesterday, I'd noticed, he'd moved the urn to the window ledge where the cat had always sat. I could feel its presence as I swept.

I remembered how Clio had incorporated the cat into the background of her "before" garden sketch. She'd never drawn the "after." I stopped for a moment and leaned on the broom and gazed over the forlorn spot. How it had changed. This was the death of after.

Once dinner was over I got out my nail polish and got started on the evening's entertainment. I couldn't go to the Short Stop anymore, not since I'd been pegged by the cops. But that was okay. They'd lost me anyway when they'd dropped my beer. I had my Simenon map and books and Bach.

I started to feel better by the time the third beer hit. The bungalow held onto the heat of the day. I had to replace my fluids.

I was working on one of my favorite books and got sidetracked rereading passages, so it was nearly ten when I finally called it a night. I remounted the map on the wall, above the shrine to Clio, adjusting its pitch a couple times until it hung just right. I stepped back and admired my handiwork. The map was a constellation of bright enamel dots.

I stretched the length of my body, conscious again of the stifling atmosphere. I wouldn't be able to sleep tonight, the deep dreamless sleep I needed. I moved the fan around the room, but it was a hopeless effort. Inside, there wasn't a breath of air. Outside would be better.

But the steps of the stoop still radiated, so I padded to the far end of the court where the concrete stopped and sat down in the empty lot. This was good, I thought — and would be even better once I got rid of whatever was pinching my crotch. I reached into my pocket and pulled out June Barry's calling card. I'd forgotten I'd been carrying it around the last few days.

It was much cooler here. A breeze rustled the leaves of the avocado. I fingered the card, flipped it slowly over and over in my hand before replacing it in my pocket.

I knew who it was when I heard the steps coming down the court. I knew the gait. I knew the walk. I knew the sound of her car engine. She sat down beside me without a word; I didn't add two cents. We were the only ones silent, it seemed, as the cool air washed over the slope of the hill, triggering a shiver of wind chimes. From the top of the avocado a mockingbird let loose a warble. Crickets rubbed their wings at our feet. High above the empty lot, above the city lights, a harvest moon traveled slowly across the heavens along with a blimp selling tires.

Closer to home space was at a standstill: our fingers, inches from each other, untouching. Only the breeze moved through the court, on its back a waft of lavender.